Schizophrenia

Bruce Buckner

First Edition
ISBN Paperback 979-8-9855658-3-6
Copyright © 2022 by Bruce Buckner

Bruce Buckner,Inc
www.BruceBuckner.com

Table of Contents

PROLOGUE

-Marcus-

"I take it that I'm supposed to commit the murder that Det. Pike wanted?" I assumed with my anger coming to a boil.

"Yes, I tried to stop him, but he refused and threatened to ruin my career, and possibly take my life if I said anything about it.

"You mean, Chucky?" I asked in disbelief.

"Yes, I'm so sorry Marcus. Please forgive me." Ashley continued to cry. I said nothing as I stood. My abrupt actions alarmed her.

"Wait, Marcus where are you going?" she grabbed my arm with pleading eyes.

"Don't touch me you snake bitch!" I snatched my arm away looking down at her with pure conviction in my eyes.

"Please Marcus, let him be… Chucky isn't worth losing your life over" Ashley pleaded.

"He won't be alive to talk about it. The only way I'll be caught is if you tell. Then again, you won't be alive either." Without another word, I whipped out my clock and placed it to her head (Boom!) Her brains splattered across the couch. I tucked the pistol and grabbed my Jacket. Just then, the phone rang. I let it ring until the answering machine picked up.

{Hey Ashley, this is chucky. I know we aren't on good terms, but I'm in jail. I stepped out my hideout and Detectives were instructed to hold me until Det. Pike got here, but I don't know why. Please help me Ash. Beep.}

I thought to myself that Chucky had a lot of nerve to even fathom Ashley helping after the predicament he put her in. I picked up the phone and dialed 911, leaving it off the hook. I grabbed the keys to Ashley's Acura and gave her one last look before making my exit. Once outside, I instinctively snatched the 40 off my waist. Marcel was leaning on Ashley's Acura clapping his hands.

"Bravo, young Marcus. Bravo. Two shots, two kills. One gun! You're getting good my friend. You're starting to kill on instinct and without thought." Marcell spoke candidly. I took aim and made an aggressive advance.

"How the fuck you know I was here?" I questioned after hearing about Chucky I didn't know who to trust.

"Damn, you really were slipping. I followed you here from the apartment. That was a brave thing you did, killing that cop. It was also smart. I don't understand why you killed Ashley though, she was a good bitch!" Marcell lit up a Newport.

"How do you know I killed them?" I asked, pistol aimed. He then pointed to the open living room blinds sitting wide-open.

"Look Marcus, I'm with you not against you. I'm in this much as you are. Tell me what the fuck is going on." He stated. I lowered my pistol seeing that he was right.

"Ashley and Chucky was trying to set me up with pike. They were trying to make it so Pike caught me in the act. That's why I killed Ashley. Det. Pike just so happened to come over. I killed him while I had the chance."

"I told you that nigga was working." He slammed his cigarette by the thought.

"Look man, we gotta move the police gonna be here soon. We can talk in the car." I hopped in the Acura with Marcell following suite and sped off. "That's explains how Pike knew I was at the Child Advocacy building. Ashley found a conscience and tried to help me but it was too much of a risk to let her live." I could already feel that Ashley's murder would bother me later.

"Alright, so let's go get that nigga Chucky." Marcell, eager to kill.

"Not yet! He's locked up. I left him at the apartment and he tried to go to his apartment, and got bagged. Police gonna find Det. Pike body in minute. When it goes public, hopefully whatever surveillance on Terrica Barr will leave. Pike is the head! Once you cut off the head, the body will crumble. Right now, we just gotta wait everything out." I explained.

"It's your show Marky. I'm just a character in it" Marcell replied and lit other Newport.

Chapter 1

14 Years Prior

-Marcus-

I woke up drenched in sweat. By now, I was used to it. My dreams were always the same. Not to mention, that I always awoke when Marcell killed my mother. For the past seven years, it's been hard for me to talk about that night. It was weird to me because I dreamed about it almost every night. It happened so much that it became normal to me. Maybe it was my good memories that got me through the six life sentences I was serving. Even at this very moment, I laid on my slab of a brick for a bed in a deep reverie, musing about my past.

"Hell no you can't have no money. Get the fuck out my face." That was Karen to most people; but to me she was my mother. Up until her death seven years ago, she'd always been the same invective woman about everything.

"I can't even remember hearing a compliment or any pleasantry come out of her mouth. Still, she loved me as her son. At least I hoped and thought that she did. Although her action said otherwise. Through it all, she was still my mother. I would love her with my entire essence. With me being the only child, one would think that I was spoiled. That wasn't the case in my household. I was lucky to get a simple thank you at times for all the work I was forced to do. I never knew my dad. My mother would never talk about him and would get mad if I asked, so I simply discarded the thought of the man I never knew.

My name is Marcus Tidwell; and this is my story verses the theory of the D.C government, and how I allegedly killed my mother.

Today marked ten years since that tragic night. This will be the first time I have given my side of that horrible event. It took me this long to be able to re-live the beginning of the destruction of my life. Today I would, and I would do it from the Peace and Serenity of my cell. I've strategically choose to do it from here, because for the past three years I've sat in solitude with no one to keep me company, but mind. Kind of like learned behavior, because from age 12 to 19 that's all I had to keep me company anyway. Well, that and Marcell, I'll get back to him later.

It all began when I was 12 years old. It was freezing outside and snow was falling freely. I was attending Paul Middle School in Northwest Washington D.C. I sat in class with my eyes darting out the window at the sea of white. Then back to the clock reading 3:12 pm.

"Three more minutes," I said to myself. I was good at school, but like most kids would rather play video games or watch cartoons. With my mind on all I wanted to do when I got home, the three minutes felt like seconds. Then like music to my ears, the school bell rung ending the school day. I ran to retrieve my book bag from my locker anxious to get home. Just as I closed my locker, my best friend approached.

"What's up Marcus? What are you doing after school?" That was my friend Chucky. We've been attending the same school since elementary. From letters to numbers. Chucky was of a light complexion with deep red freckles. The other kids used to pick on him, and call him a Dalmatian. Not me, I saw Chucky for the good dude he truly was. Besides, I was never one to follow crowd.

"After I do my homework, I can come out, why?" I tucked my thumbs through the straps of my book bag.

"I was talking to Ashley today and she said we can come over her house because her parents aren't going to be there. So you know what that mean." Chucky smiled devilishly. Ashley was arguably the prettiest girl in the school, and the most promiscuous in same. For a young guy, with little experience, you'd gain some real fast dealing with Ashley. Not to mention, she was 14 years old.

"In most case my homework can wait. I still need to go home and check in with my mom, but after that we can go." My mind began to turn with all the possibilities that the visits could produce.

"Alright then, cool. I'll go check in with my mom and we will meet back up at *The Wings And Things*. Be there at 4:00

pm." Chucky instructed. With that, Chucky and I made our way home. We both lived on a street called KDY. That was short for Kennedy St. although KDY was surrounding by houses, it still belonged to low-income families. Crime reigned victorious with living conditions like that, a child growing up would almost have no choice but to adapt to his surrounding and go for self.

The walk home was short like the norm and we both had our minds set on Ashley. Anxious, was an understatement. I almost had an anxiety attack in my pants just thinking about her.

"Don't forget; be at *The Wings and Things* at 4:00 pm." Chucky reminded me. Little did he know I didn't need to be reminded of anything.

I'll be there; you just make sure you are." I pointed for emphasis. Chucky and I parted ways with our plans etched in stone. Walking on the seventh street, I looked in the distance and saw the White Denali parked a few doors down from my house. Its owner was a guy named Pearl.

"Pearl was a known Pimp residing in Northwest, but was supposedly internationally known and respected. He stood at 6'0 feet with a red complexion, curly hair and hazel eyes. That pretty motherfucker made Pearl one deceptive predator. Pretty on the outside, cold as ice to the core. The fear he instilled in everyone produced the return effect of respect in all aspects. Everyone but me, I despised him and his ways.

Pearl, at the time had been with my mother for a few months. I knew he was no good from the start. He wasn't the first man my mother brought home to me. All the others made it they're sole priority to placate me in anyway that they could. They understood that the way to my mother was to go through me. Basically saying, we were a package deal. Ultimately, the men made sure to establish a booming relationship with me to win my mom over. They all never stayed long. My mom was a tough cookie, with her mean ass.

Pearl on the other hand was different. He showed genuine qualities about himself that he was a completely new type of *Asshole*. That motherfucker didn't show me any type of interest at all. That led me to believe that he was only interested in two things money and pussy. I don't know if Pearl was pimping my mother, but she didn't have a problem paying the bills.

Recently my mom got sick and was forced to be bed ridden until she got better. I walked in the house hearing Pearl yelling at my mom. "What the fuck you mean you're sick bitch. You making me lose money because your bitch ass sick." Pearl expressed his anger. I crept up the stairs in time to witness Pearl taking off his belt.

"You one lazy bitch, Karen. Don't worry though, I got something for you lazy ass. You gonna pay for making *Pearly White* lose money." Pearl wrapped his belt around his hand.

"Please, Pearl, I'll go. I'll work Pearl, I'll do it." She pleaded. It hurt me to my heart to hear my mother begging this motherfucker for mercy. I watched as my mother cries were ignored. Pearl cocked back sending it crashing across my mother face.

"Aggghhh." She fell back against the headboard holding her stinging face. Continuously Pearl beat my mother. I cringed with every blow that he delivered. He beat her so much that after a while it looked as if she became immune to the abuse, and just lay there. Pearl then dropped the belt and began to undo his pants. Softly my mother cried.

'Fucking with Ol' Pearl money is a no-no, bitch! You gotta learn your lesson"

"Please Pearl, I'll make it up. Please." She softly pleaded.

"Naw, bitch, you gonna make nit up right here and now." Pearl removed his pear-handled, 45 automatic from the hostler in the small of his back. I watched as he place it in the bed next to him. His back was to me as he stood in front of the bed. Pearl dropped his pant and boxers. Upon seeing Pearls hard penis fully erect, my mother began to frantically plead already knowing what was the inevitable.

"No please, Pearl, I'll work harder. Please don't do this." Pearl said nothing as he grabbed my mother by the knees. Aggressively, he spread her legs. Karen began a feeble fight even if only to save her womanhood only for one day. But it was futile. Pearl was too strong, and easily forced his way between her thighs.

"Oh god no, please Pearl, Arrrrrggghhhh." She screamed out in agonizing pain as Pearls hardened penis ripped through her walls. Finally, I could take nor hear any more. I gathered all the strength in my young body and bolted towards Pearls gun. Before he realized what was going on I was clutching the heavy weapon with both hand aiming at his chest. The crazy part was the look he gave me. Even with the deadly weapon pointing at him, he was still the same invective man I knew him to be. He stood there chest poked out and as he *Intrepid* as a man could be.

"You playing a big man's game little Marcus. Better put my gun down before I do you like I was just doing your mother here." Pearl spoke placidly, and smiled as if he wasn't staring down a barbell.

"I ain't putting shit down. You better leave my mother alone." I was filled with fear. Not from Pearl, but from what I might do to Pearl. I was prepare to defend my mother to death if need be. With my defiance spoken an eerie silence feel into the room. Both, mines and Pearls eyes locked on one another's. Suddenly, Pearl lunged at me. Frightened I rapidly squeezed the trigger, I didn't take aim, so I prayed the shots hits the intended target.

"By the time I stopped squeezing the trigger the room was again deafly quite. Pearl laid face down in a pool of his own blood. My mother sat up looking at Pearl's dead body in disbelief, I expected her to run to me for comfort, but that wasn't the case.

"Nooo, you bastard. You killed him. You fucking bastard." She yelled then rushed me with a right hook. I fell to the floor holding my face. The word confused couldn't express how I felt at the very moment. My mind was so distorted that although I was awake it felt as though I were losing time. Like I blacked out but my eyes were wide open.

"Oh my God, Pearl, hold on I'm gonna get you some help" I watched her rub his head as she called 911. "I need help my son just shot my boyfriend. Please I need help and bring the police, I want my son arrested for this." I couldn't believe my ears. My own mother called the police on me. Then everything went black and I awoke in a small room shackled to the floor. I didn't remember how I got there or where I was. If the Governments theory was right, this was around the time that I met Marcell.

I later found out that the officer took me to the Homicide Division on Branch Ave. I sat in the same room for hours. At times, I would look out the door window, but rarely saw anyone that I was familiar with. The way the police treated me you'd think I was a hardened criminal. I'd be the first to admit that with all that was happening and happened I was scared. Soon, I heard my mom talking to an officer outside of the door.

"Ma'am since he's a minor we're gonna need you to sign these paper authorizing us to speak with him." The fat Detective stated.

"Look here, Detective, and I want to make myself very clear when I say this. That little motherfucker in there." She pointed at me. "I don't want him, I ain't been happy since the day he jumped out of my pussy. Then he kills the only man who loved me since I can remember. Let the state have him." Hearing her words crushed me. I thought my mother just had problems showing me love but in reality, she hated me. I didn't know what to feel. What to think? All I did know was that through it all I still loved that woman more than life itself.

"I'm sorry ma'am, but you're asking me to do something outside of my job description. I'm an investigating Detective, not a Child Advocate. Now as I said, I need your signature so that I may continue this case. If not, everything stops." My mother snatched the papers from him in an aggressive manner and signed them. She then threw the papers to his chest.

"If it ain't your description, then find someone whose it is. Until then he's yours. I'm leaving. Call me when you ready to prosecute his ass." My mother gave me one last look then left me in the presence of this stranger. The detective took a deep breath and entered the room. As he sat, he wiped his brow with a napkin and said something that I'll never forget.

"Do you have any other relative in this D.C., Maryland or Virginia area?" I couldn't respond. I simply buried my face in my arms as I realized that I'd just become *State Property*.

Soon I was taken to the Oakhill Youth center to await trial. While there, I was appointed a Child Advocate to oversee my case. Her name was Terrica Barr. She was always nice to me and gave me hugs where she pressed my head against her large breast. I grew to trust her more than anyone at that time in my life. A mistake in itself.

A few weeks later, I got a legal visit from a person who looked a lot like Bill Clinton. My first mind told me don't trust him, but Ms. Barr was there and told me that it was okay. Reluctantly, I took a seat inside the small room.

"Hello Marcus, my name is Thomas Kennedy. I'm going to be your lawyer." He gave me a smile that looked more devious than good. Nor was it contagious.

"I wanna go home." I flatly stated.

"I'm sure you do Marcus. That is what I'm here for, to get you home." He placed a hand on my shoulder.

"you're a liar. How the hell am I going home when my mom doesn't want me." I pushed his hand away and stood from my chair. "Ms. Barr, I don't want to be here." I said in a demanding nature. She sensed my anger and pulled me into the hallway.

"Now Marcus I want you to listen to me and give this man a chance. He may not be able to get you back home with your mom, but he damn sure can get this murder off your back... and get you out of here. Now I want you to go get a soda out the machine and come back. At least just to hear him out." She handed me a dollar.

"How do you expect me to do that; when he's lying to me already?" I replied in disbelief.

"What did I say, Marcus?. She grabbed my chin.

"Alright, alright, Damn."

"And watch your mouth boy!" she lightly popped me in the head. I sucked my teeth and went to get my soda. I made it back to the room in a little less than five-minutes. As I walked in, I saw Mr. Kennedy taking his hands out of Ms. Barr's pants. I acted like I didn't see it and took a seat near Ms. Barr.

Mr. Kennedy talked a good game. I really believed that he could not only get me home, but out of trouble for killing Pearl. Kennedy came to see me once a week for two months. Let him tell it, he had been working hard on my case. I later found out that was not of any truth.

Today was like any other visit from Kennedy. I walked in the room where he and Ms. Barr sat. When I stepped in the room, Ms. Barr walked toward me with tears streaming down her face. She embraced me pressing my head against her breast.

"What's wrong, Ms. Barr?" I asked. She looked to Mr. Kennedy who gave her a stern look.

"It's nothing! I'm alright." She replied, but wouldn't look at me. I then took my seat.

"How you holding up in here buddy." Mr. Kennedy shook my hand.

"I'm good!" I smiled.

"Well, I got some good news for you," he slid me a pen and a document. "You're getting out of here. This paper is to say that you were just protecting your mom. When you sign that, we'll go to court tomorrow for the judge to release you." He said that shit with a straight face but I later learned that was a bold face lie.

"With my mom?" I looked up as I asked, voice filled with optimism.

"Well not with your mom, but Uhh… you can live with Ms. Barr." Ms. Barr gave him a glare that spoke a thousand words. I was ecstatic. I was going to be a free man again and nothing else mattered.

"Where do I sigh?" I was smiling from ear to ear.

"Right there!" He pointed. After I signed, he took it and handed it to Ms. Barr whom started to cry as she signed it as well.

"That's it Marcus. You can go back to your room, and I'll see you at court tomorrow."

"Thank you for everything, Mr. Kennedy, and you too Ms. Barr." I stepped around the table and gave them both a hug before returning to my unit. As I left, I looked back at the room to Mr. Kennedy hugging Ms. Barr as she cried into his shoulder. At that point I could care less. I was going home. Tomorrow could not have come quicker. When it did nothing was what I expected it to be.

-Marcus-

Marcus Devon Tidwell, I accept your guilty plea and sentence you to Juvenile Life with an R to the custody of the Department of Justice for Juvenile's. I pray that after your time that you learn that guns are not for kids." He then banged the gavel and the Marshal stepped up and grabbed my arm

"This way son! He spoke. By the Judges words, I became frantic.

"What! Where am I going? I signed the paper. I'm supposed to be going home." I became frantic. "Tell him Mr. Kennedy, tell him." He put his head down.

"I'm sorry Marcus." He replied then gathered his things.

"No tell 'em, Mr. Kennedy." I looked to the crowd for Ms. Barr. Once I found her, she looked down and wiped her tears away with the back of her hand. The Marshal continued to push me towards the back. At that time, I thought I would be in jail for the rest of my life.

As soon as I got back to Oakhill, they switched my unit. I went from being housed detainee, to being committed. I couldn't see nothing but my fresh Life Sentence I had. When I walked in the unit, all eyes were on me. I could honestly say that I was scared to death.

"What is your name son?" A big black counselor asked.

"Marcus." I replied slightly poking my chest out.

"Marcus what?" His deep baritone voice resounded.

"Tidwell, Marcus Tidwell."

"Alright, Marcus Tidwell, follow me, and I will show you your room." As I followed him, everyone had their eyes on me… So I had my eyes on them. Although I was scared, I refused to show it.

"Bed must be made by seven. Count 7:30 am. Breakfast is at eight." I said nothing. I just walked in and lay on my bunk. Just as he left, a light-skinned guy slid in and lay on the floor next to my bed. His head propped up on his elbow. "What's up Marcus?"

"Who the fuck is you?" I stated.

"The names Marcell and yours is Marcus." He stated and I stood up in case I had to protect myself.

"How do you know my name?" I was at a lost for words.

"I'm psychic. Sike, Naw, I heard you tell Mr. Brick your name."

"That's Mr. Bricks?" I pointed to the counselor.

"Yeah, What you in for?"

"Murder!" I said with a slight hint of aggression and lay back down.

"So am I, I got Life with an "R". What about you?" Marcell asked.

"Same thing."

"What! How the hell you get Life with an "R". I saw your case in the paper. That shit was self-defense all day in the paint.

"Tell me about it. My lawyer tricked me into signing a plea deal. Had me thinking I was going home."

"Them Public Pretenders some dirty motherfuckers. Somebody need to kill that dirty motherfucker." Marcell suggested.

"You right about that." I replied.

"How old are you, Marcus?" Marcell asked,

"12, but I'm almost 13. What about you?

"17 and my "R" about to come off. Once that happen, I'm blowing this Popsicle Stand. By the way, if you're serious about killing that lawyer I can help make that happen as well.

"You'd do that for me?" I looked at him.

"Why not, we're cellies now. We're in this together. You got my back and I got yours" Marcell replied and held out a fist for a pound. I guess as a form of acceptance I hit his fist like that Judge banged his gavel on my ass.

"No question!" From that point on Marcell became two peas in the pod. Literally!

Chapter 2

-Marcus-

(7 years later)

After about a year Marcell told me that he got his "R" removed. Soon after he was gone. Even though he left he still kept in contact with me. I'd get at least one letter a week. My name didn't get called at mail call. But somehow when I get a letter from him it magically appeared in my room. We talked about everything, but mostly about exacting my revenge on Kennedy and Ms. Barr.

I sat on my bunk reading a letter from Marcell. I re-read a sentence repeatedly until it etched in my mind. *Everyone who crossed us will pay for it.* I didn't know exactly what Marcell was capable of, but I did know that he was dangerous. My thoughts were broken by a loud rapport on my door.

"Tidwell, you ready?" your check out time is here." Mr. Brick informed. Today was my release date for killing Pearl. I was happy to be going home, but I didn't know what my future held. The only future I knew was that of Thomas Kennedy and Terrica Barr.

"Yeah, I'm, ready." I replied. I quickly gathered my things and took one last look at the place that I called home for the past seven years. I was escorted by three counselors from my cell to release and delivery. I've travelled down a long road since I killed Pearl. Now being released I wasn't gonna look back.

"Once I made it to the front of the building, I could feel the atmosphere change. The air smelled different. It was the smell of freedom. The smell of having the will power to exact justice from injustice the city of Washington had caused me. I took a deep breath and stepped through the threshold.

After about ten steps, I turned around to take in the structure that held me captive for the past seven years. Barbwire covered every edge with one way in and one way out. It was hell within brick and steel. Feeling that I'd seen enough of that hellhole, I turned my back to it ready to put it behind me. As I did a money-green BMW pulled up. At first, I didn't know what to make of it, so I stood there. The BMW stopped dead in front of me. Its tint were very dark, making it impossible to see who was driving. Gradually, the sunroof opened. Then like a jack in the box Chucky popped up

"Marky, Mark! Welcome home, baby." Chucky held a big smile on his face that was contagious to point it found itself on mines.

"Well if it isn't Charles Lee Ray." I joked, calling him by Chucky's real name in the movie *Child's Play*.

"I thought I told you in my last letter I wanted to catch the bus home?'

"How could I let my right hand man ride the bus home when I'm pushing this pretty motherfucker?" Chucky waved a hand of presentation looking the luxury car over in admiration. "You better come on before those people change their mind." Chucky slightly laughed. Seeing his logic, I hurried and got in the car. Quickly Chucky sped off. I was happy to see Chucky. Besides Marcell, he was the only one I kept contact with for the past seven years. Not to mention another person I've talked to about my murderous aspirations.

"So what's up Marcus, you still wanna get at that Lawyer and that Advocate?" Chucky bluntly asked.

"Without question!" I replied then looked at him. What, you having cold feet? I got serious.

"Not even, say no more my comrade. The future is ahead of us, so let's make society pay you back for the debt that's owed to you." His words calmed my nerves. "There's a lot you missed and a lot you have to learn my man." Chucky briefly looked at me.

"Yeah I missed a lot." I stared out the window.

"When was the last time you spoke with your mother?" Chucky cut his eyes at me again. The question caught me off guard. My mother was a chapter in my book of life that I wasn't ready to open until I became face to face with her. I wasn't about to deter myself from that just for Chucky's natural curiosity. To be as laconic as I could, would have to satisfy his curiosity appetite.

"I haven't. Talk about something else." I insisted. Chucky caught the hint. He already knew my mother was a touchy subject. Respectfully, he respected it.

"What about money, what you plan on doing for money?" Again, he cut his eyes at me.

"I haven't thought much about it, but I take it you have." Still I stared out the window. I was thinking how much D.C had changed. I looked over at Chucky with a smile plastered on my face. I could tell by his line of questioning he really did have something in mind.

"No question, slim. I know you don't think this car came from legitimate money because it sure as hell didn't." Chucky laughed.

'I've made that assumption already, so what exactly are you into?" I flatly asked.

"Mainly, PCP but a little of everything. The streets have treated me good. I've been at it five years with no arrest. I gotta be doing something right. Now you home, I can show you the ends and outs. There's a lot of money to be made. We just have to apply ourselves and get it. Basic math, you hear me.' Chucky looked at me and smiled. Oh, Yeah, and this is for you." Chucky retrieved a box off the backseat and place it on my lap.

"What is this?" I looked down at it, not really attempting to guess what was inside.

"Open it nigga!" Chucky edged. I lifting the lid revealed a 9mm and a cell phone.

"That's all you. You gonna need that heat out here. Everyone using cell phones so it's only right you come home to one of your own."

"Thanks Chuck." I placed the gun on the floor under my feet and turned on the phone." Just like that, I was back at it.

I was stared out the window taking in my hometown more than anything that chucky was saying. My mind was on everything and everyone who oppressed and sent me away. I just prayed when the time came that I have enough courage to handle my business.

"It wasn't long before Chucky was turning off of Georgia Avenue, and onto Kennedy Street. I could see that *Northwest* had changed a lot. Chucky continued to ramble, but my mind wasn't registering his words. Seventh and Kennedy although hadn't change a bit as far as the houses. What did change was the homeless people and the flock of junkies scattered about. The same caliber of people who lured Chucky into the street life. The ten or twenty dollar they would bring in exchange for their drug would eventually add up. Ultimately, that had to cause the hunger for more, more prevalent than the hunger for food.

I understood Chuck's aspirations. Not sure I'd partake in them as he expected, but I understood his choice. In my mind, understanding was the key to everything.

Being in the area where it all started slightly disturbed me. It forced me to relive memories that had sine been buried in the deepest bellows of my mind. I sat with my thought scattered to the point that I didn't remember Chucky parking. My eyes were glued to the house that I grew up in. I guess Chucky could sense my apprehension, so he sat quietly. I was grateful for that because I had to sort things out on my own. Especially, before I was able to confront my past head on.

"Is she home?" I asked with reluctance in my voice. My eyes glued to the structure as if I were absorbing its entirety,

"She drives that White Navigator in front of us." Chucky pointed. Again, the car fell into a deep silence. I wasn't sure if I was ready for the confrontation, but knew that becoming fully prepared was something that could take a lifetime to do.

Life was short, and it had been seven years. The time was before me, and I felt that if I didn't act now and confront my fears head on that I'd run from them forever.

"You want me to come with you?" Chucky looked over with keen sincerity.

"No!" I said a little too fast for my liking. "This is something that I have to do on my own, I'll see you later on." With that, I gathered my things without professing another word. I opened the door letting the brisk autumn air cool my face. The air of freedom was still euphoric to me. My courage had risen, pushing one foot in front of the other. Before I knew it, I was on the porch. The screen door was closed, but the front door was open. I took a deep sigh as if to say *Here we go.* I opened the screen and stepped inside allowing the screen door to slam shut. By the noise, it caused my mother, Karen to step out of the kitchen. On sight of me, she stopped in her tracks instantly recognizing me. At first, I thought I saw a smile, but her face kept moving into a face of disdain. I'd hope she'd run to me, but that wasn't the case.

"Karen made a U-turn into the living room. I started to think that it may have been a mistake to come here. But I was here, and willingly to see this confrontation all the way through. I moved through the house in search of not only my mother, but her reasoning as well. And my understanding.

Before I made it to the living room, I could already smell the burning tobacco. I turned into the living room to Karen sitting in a chair sucking on a Newport. Her knees, crossed and shaking. She looked nervous. I slowly walked towards her falling to my knees with my eyes watering. I attempted to look her in the eye but she avoided my glare as if it were burning a hole straight through her. I grabbed her hand. By my touch, she released a shaken sigh. The smoke sporadically escaped her lips.

"It's me… it's me momma." I continued through rubber lips. She gave no replay, yet rocked back and forth staring into oblivion. I could tell that this was just as hard for her as it was for me. Slowly, a lone tear cascaded down her left cheek dripping off her chin. That tear confused me because I could not decipher whether it was of happiness, or resentment. Through it all, I still loved her, but wasn't sure if she loved me the same. Finally, she turned her head and looked at me. I began to smile, but soon learned that my smile did not fit the occasion.

"Why are you here?" She asked in a voice that was cold and emotionless. As quickly as the smile spread across my face, it was gone. I could feel nothing but rejection pouring from this woman.

"I'm free Momma, I'm free. They let me go momma, I'm home." My voice, shook as I struggled to contract my words. I stared up in her brown face with my own eyes continuing to water. I was happy to be free and once again reunited with her. *Why wasn't she feeling the same?*

"I know that Marcus, but why you here." She pointed to the floor. *"In My House!"* she asked in a rising tone of anger. Not sure what she meant, I changed the subject.

"Momma why didn't you ever come to visit me?" I was already blinking away my tears.

"Because I didn't give two shits that you were there; that's why. Now why did you come here, Marcus? Her words were unremorseful with a tongue untamed.

"I,I,I live here momma" I replied in the tone of a plea verses the simple answering of her question.

"NO! You used to live here" she slammed the Newport in the ashtray. Her action drew my attention to a table filled with bottles of medication. Each bottle individually numbered.

"I don't want you here, Marcus. It's because of you that I have what I have. Your home is no longer with me." She continued. Her tongue striking me, like a double edge sword. My tears became impossible to blink away. They began to fall as free as a feather through the wind.

"I want you out!" She yelled while pointing and standing, I still sat atop of my knee submissively. When she stood, I saw that she couldn't weigh more than a hundred pounds. In a last resort to keep this woman, even along with her wicked ways I hugged her thighs.

"No momma, please. Please don't leave me." My vision blurred from the abundance of tears falling from their respective ducts.

"I said NO! She yelled using all her strength to wiggle free to no avail. I continued to hold her tight out of no where her palm crashed down across my cheeks. "I said I want you out" the blow caused me to release my grip. She backed up and pointed to the door.

"Marcus, get the hell out of my house!" she screamed with urgency. I stood to my feet easily lowering over her small frame.

"But momma, I love you" I stared in a whisper as I reached out to nothing but air.

"Well I don't Love you. In fact I don't think I have ever loved you. From the day you were born. I've cursed that day ever since you killed pearl." Her words cut a hot knife through butter. "Now get out of my house." She took steps towards me pushing me towards the front door.

"Out, Marcus! Get the fuck out of my house" She continued to push and hang her small fist on my chest.

"Please momma" I pleaded. She said nothing and opened the screen door.

"This is no longer your home." She sent another crashing blow across my cheek with the door being slammed in my face. After it all came down, I guess I finally realized my mother didn't love me. I turned from the porch and took off running in pain and mental anguish. I had no destination and no idea what I was running from, but I couldn't stop. The more I ran, the harder I cried. I turned into the alley and tripped over poorly laid asphalt. My palms scraped the cold ground. The gun fell from my waist about ten yards in front of me. Once I saw it, my first thought was End it all. As quick as I could crawl to it. I cocked it back lodging one into the chamber. Without hesitation, I placed the gun to my own head. Boom! Chucky kicked it from my hand causing it to discharge a round.

"Nooo!" I tried to crawl towards it but Chucky jumped on my back ultimately wrapping me in his arms.

"Come on Marcus, pull it together it ain't worth it man. Let it go, man. Let it go! Let her go! He said, I slowly stopped fighting and lay in his arms crying my eyes out. I felt alone now, and the only one who could change that was Karen. I don't remember when I close my eyes, but I did at some point. When it happened it was like suddenly all my mental pain and anguish dissipated.

➤ Schizophrenia

Chapter 3

-Marcell-

I rose from the couch stretching my arms in the air like a cat would on the floor. I thought of Marcus being free at last and the totality of it all. A smile spread across my face as the thoughts began to manifest. I made plans to go holla at him. Now that he was home, it was time me and him had a sit down.

Marcus was like a brother to me. Always had been if you ask me, we were closer than brothers. I'd even kill for him. Thinking about it, if my thoughts showed me favor I would have to. The bond we shared could never be broken. Only death could separate us. That was a fact that far outweighed any statement.

When I finally stood, the first thing on my mind was clothes! I made my way to the bathroom and took care of my hygiene and a quick shower. I walked in the master bedroom straight for the closet. I hoped I could find something suitable to my taste. Opening the door I was greeted by the latest fashions from Hugo Boss. Sabjato, Polo, and so on. It was easy to find a fit for tonight. I choose some blue Guess jeans, Blue and white Prada boots with a polo button up. Not too flashy, was how I thought.

After dressing I looked at the clock reading 1:30am. I grabbed my nine and was out the door to see what the streets of Washington D.C. had to offer me tonight. Just as I made it to the building front, low and behold Marcus was lighting up a Newport on the front steps.

"Well, well, well if it isn't Marcus Tidwell. Welcome home dude." I embraced him.

"Marcell! What's up nigga? What you doing around here?" he stood and gave me a hug.

"Nothing much still getting used to this freedom thing."

"You know I saw my mom when I got out?" Marcus mood turn into a somber one.

"Aw man, don't start that. You need to stop stressing about someone who ain't stressing about you. You saw her, and I did too. Look how skinny she got. Hell, she looked like she one bad cold away from seeing God's heavenly angel's" I tried to reason with him.

"You're right, but she's still my mother, and if she sick I'm gonna take care of her" Marcus defended the woman who bore him.

"You know what Marcus, You one stupid motherfucker. That bitch locked your ass up in that hellhole and left you for dead for seven years. Even still, you defended her like she Mary fucking Magdalene. I'm out! Fuck you, and that HIV carrying bitch!" I walked off the front fuming at how blind Marcus was. Eventually, I looked back but he was gone. Pissed off was an understatement. I needed a stress reliever and knew just how to get one.

I had to walk for a while but eventually found what I was looking for. A Crown Victoria Police Package. I hadn't hotwired a car in about seven years, but for me it was like a walk in the park. I got it started in 5 seconds flat. The speakers instantly came to life blaring the sounds of Tupac, Hit'em up. Feeling that my mood was matched I threw the car in reverse and backed out into traffic. Before long, I was cruising with a gangster lean and one hand on the stirring wheel.

The D.C. night-lights shone bright, and I was in a placid mood making it easier for my mind to contemplate my future moves and murders. Now was time for me. All me no sharing. Just me against the world or at least against D.C. I considered myself to be an animalistic man with ways one in the same. My nuts were calling, so tonight would strictly be to placate my savage sexual hunger.

I could see the sign shinning bright as in turned the corner. The stadium was the name it displayed out front. The streets were crowded with patrons of the club. Some enjoying the night, some was stumbling from excessive drinking *Loafin'* was what I called it. Them drunk bastards wouldn't smell a stickup kid or a rival enemy. They'd be dead before they could slur the word *Help!*

I turned into the parking lot, my head light shining on the patrons. As I pulled in the patrons began to scatter out of the way. Still in my shoulder lean, I let the car ease to a slow creep all the way into the parking lot. I know I wouldn't be able to carry my nine inside, so I left it under the seat. I stepped out the Crown Vic. brushing imaginary lint off my shoulder. I felt like the world was in my palm, and I was the only one in it.

I could fell different pairs of eyes stabbing me from different directions. I had that *just coming home glow* and knew it. I made it the front door stepping inside like the patrons were waiting on my arrival. Three steps in I felt a massive hand wrap around my arm. I felt my temper rising instantly. I looked up in search of the culprit. The hand belonging to a mammoth sized bouncer. He had to be every bit of 6'4 300lbs. black as tar with a handle bar moustache. With his black shirt coupled with his skin complexion, he looked like a shadow, or a thumbprint.

"Excuse me slim, what the fuck you touching me for?" I looked him up and down showing, my disgust. The bouncer smiled and willingly humbled himself.

"My apologies sir, but I need some ID." His voice was calm and deep. I then thought to myself *Damn! I had no ID, and no money to pay my way in*. I did the only thing that I could. I told him the truth.

"Look man, I'm 24 year old. I left my ID at the crib." I tried to sound as convincing as I could, but by the look of this big burley motherfucker. I could tell that he wasn't buying it at all.

"You have to step out the club sir. No ID, no entrance." He professed. Being rejected, made me feel some type of way. Under different circumstances, I would have left his big ass right where he stood. There was a time and place for everything and this wasn't the place for a murder. Knowing the carnage that I could inflict on this man life, I understood that he didn't know any better. With that little bit of understanding I humbled myself, and smiled arrogantly.

"You know what, you got this big man. 'No ID, No entrance.' Don't get your feathers all riled up." I patted him in the chest twice and made my way back outside. Back in the car, I sat frustrated from being so anxious with nothing to get into. Just when I thought all hope was lost, a white Cadillac STS pulled in the spot next to me. Its stereo playing the soft sound of Keysha Cole. I stared attentively anticipating the driver's entrance into my vision.

The door swung open and out stood the prettiest red bone I'd ever seen. Her hair was cut short in honor of Halle Barry. Automatically, I could tell she was a stripper and a dish that I must have. I knew I didn't have the experience of courtship, but I felt I was a spoiled individual and would have what I wanted. With that, I let the thrill of the chase pull me out the car to place myself in the complete presence of this woman. Our paths crossed at the tail of my vehicle.

"Excuse me miss they call me Marcell, and you?" for split second, she looked annoyed. I guess it was the sight of my politely extended hands that eased her frustration. Reluctant, but curious to my intentions, she accepted.

"Hello my name is Cream." She smiled showing receptiveness to my advance. I wondered how many times a night she gave that same smile to her abundance of customers.

"Look baby girl, I ain't gonna beat around the bush. How much do you make in a night in a place like this?" Her face became stone like then turned to business.

"What is it to you?" She shifted her body weight to one leg with a hand on her hip.

"Well I want to purchase your services for the night. Whatever you would have made tonight is what I will pay you." I revealed. I could tell her mind was spinning.

"Eleven hundred, for the night." She blurted out a little too anxiously. *I know she was probably lying but I didn't care because I wasn't planning on paying for nothing.*

"That ain't about nothing. We're taking your car or mines? I confidently asked with an arrogant smile. Confidence was the key to making anything sound feasible.

"We can take your car. Mine will be safe here. You can drop me off here in the morning."

"Sho nuff, baby girl." With that said, and the rest established, I walked around to the passenger side to open up her door. She smiled at my chivalry and took a seat inside the

Crown Victoria. Closing the door, I surveyed the area searching for any set of eyes calculating our encounter. Everyone I saw was lost in their own world, oblivious to the abduction being committed right before their eyes.

I pulled out of the parking lot gradually enough not to set off any consternations abroad. Throughout the ride, I remained relatively quiet. Occasionally, Cream luscious thighs with Zebra stripe pants would catch my eye. Although I knew I wanted her, the fact of actually having it made me nervous. I guess Cream could sense it when she reached over, palming my dick through my pants.

Her hands aroused my parts of my loins that never been aroused by another. Before I knew it, she had my pants unzipped and my dick in her hand stroking me gracefully as I drove. I'd never experienced such pleasure and wondered what more was there to offer. Cream leaned over and began sucking on my earlobe and kissing my neck. The task of driving became a task with Cream and her sexually driven antics.

"Go to the *Econo Lodge* on New York Ave." She whispered in my ear. The heat from her whisper caused my hormones to churn harder. I gave no response, but made my way straight to the Motel. I pulled into the parking lot and found the most darkened spot that I could as I parked it was as if on cue Cream leaned over and engulfed my dick down her throat. When she rose, she smiled at the sexual control that she had over me.

Desperately trying to regain my composure, I caught the Blue and White sign reading *Econo Lodge* in my peripheral. That's when it hit me; she would expect me to pay for the room. I was clueless as to what I should do. I had no ID, and absolutely no money. Meaning my cover would be blown in any minute. Then like a prayer being answered Cream pulled out a room key.

"No need to buy a room. I purchase one every night before I go to work." She smiled and got out the car. Luckily, she did or she would have saw me release a heavy sigh of release , I stylishly grabbed my nine from under the seat and tucked it on my waist. I followed behind Cream, watching her hips sway from side to side.

When we arrived at the door Cream stepped in first with me closing the rear along with the door behind me. When I turned from locking the door, Cream stood before me with her hand out and the other on her hip.

"No pay, No play!" she said with a serious look on her face. My cover was blown. It was time to lay the cards on the table. I reached on my waist and gripped my nine.

"Bitch you know what it is , strip before I kill your dumb ass. I spoke with a sinister tone. Cream realized her mistake on sight of my gun. Her mouth hung open in disbelief.

"Please don't hurt me. I don't care about the money. You can still fuck me. Just please don't hurt me." Cream held her palms up in front of her as a sign of surrender. Slowly, she backed up as if she had some type of exit.

"I wasn't paying your dumbass no way. Now don't let me say it again. Strip!" My face held no emotion. Even with the new criminal conduct, I was adapting like a seasoned Vet. Cream meticulously began to peel each individual article of clothing off her womanly curves. I couldn't help but salivate as my eyes roamed her body. My dick sat stiff as a pole.

"Turn around and bend over that bed." I demanded. Cream moved slowly towards the bed not once taking her eyes off the nine still aimed. I began to undress myself with one arm. I stepped behind her gaining a perfect view of her pussy. I set the nine on the small of her back as I positioned myself to enter her. Just as I thrust myself through her walls, I could see a lone tear cascade her cheek. The sight of her crying struck a chord in me. I snatched the pistol off her back and aimed at the back of her head.

"Wipe your face bitch, stop crying." I stated calmly.

"I, I, I, can't." A fresh wave of tears began to shoot out.

"I said wipe your fucking face!" I yelled. My anger caused Cream to jump and sob harder.

"Please!" Creamed sobbed uncontrollably.

"Stop fucking crying!" Boom! I could not take it any longer and sent a bullet through the back of her head. Still, I could see the wet streaks that tears left in her wake. I pulled out of her lifeless body and ran to the bathroom. Quickly, I returned with the tissue to wipe away the tears. Carefully, I patted her face until they were gone. Staring at the dead body, I suddenly felt that Cream looked mor beautiful dead, than alive. Unusually, this made my sexual attention towards her even greater.

I then repositioned myself behind her and jammed my dick inside her lifeless pussy. The feeling was unexplainable and the highest pleasure that I had ever experienced. The pressure inside churned hard with each strike, seconds later, I exploded inside Creams corpse. As soon as I pulled out Cream body released liquid solid waste.

"Right on time!" I spoke to myself. I quickly got dressed and turned the lights out. Stepping out of the room and back into the cool night's air I felt a thousand pounds lighter. I hopped back in the Crown Victoria and headed home.

Chapter 4

-Chucky-

I felt dotty for Marcus, and what he was enduring with his mother tearing him down and he could do nothing to stop it. Had I not chased behind him when I saw him hightail it out of the house he would have killed himself. The bad part would have been that it was all over a woman who couldn't give a breath of life if he was dying.

Once I got him together I took him to my apartment. The entire ride, which was only up the street he was out of it. All he could do was cry. If not that, he said nothing at all, staring into oblivion. Luckily, my building was just across the street. Marcus was my man, so I made myself a promise that I would help him get through his time of turmoil as much as I could. We got in my apartment and I laid him on the couch. He took the rest of his mind and body so desperately needed.

Marcus slept for the rest of the day. Since his attempted suicide, I decided to stay with him. I wanted to call Ashley over to keep me company, but I decided against it. Eventually, I ended up falling asleep to give my body the much-needed rest it required. By 12:00 am, I was awakened by my cell phone.

"What up?" I groggily answered.

"What's up. Moe. This Don I need you." Doe was one of my biggest buyers. He's from an area in Northwest called Fairmont. Because it was the norm for him to meet his needs I took the early morning call.

"This is a burn-out phone, what do you need?" slowly, I sat up thinking about money.

"I need a quarter – man, and a pound of Loud."

"Okay give me ten." I replied.

"Bet! Meet me around Fairmont."

"Come on "S", you know I don't like coming around there. Its hot ass shit around there. Not to mention, ya'll still beefing with "35"

"Man, if you don't bring your scary ass around here. Ain't nothing gonna happen to you nigga." He assured weightlessly.

"Alright I'm coming, but next time you coming to me."

"Alright call me when you around here." *Click!* He hung up, and I continued to get dressed. I weighed out quarter brick of Coke on a digital and placed it on the scale then into a zip lock bag. After doing the same to the Loud, I tossed my leather on and tucked my Glock on my waist. I grabbed my car keys, checked on Marcus, and I was out the door. Leaving him to his dreams. I figured that I would be back in about thirty minutes or so.

I stepped into the brisk night air adjusting my pistol as I made my way to the parking lot. My BMW sparked in the moon light. I walked passed it to my Navy blue Riviera. In the profession that I was in, a dirt car was necessary. I tossed the lock bag with the work on the passenger seat, and my Glock on my lap. The stereo blared the soft sound of Kenistry. Gradually, I pulled out the parking lot on route to Fairmont.

As soon as I turned off 14th street and onto Fairmont and eerie feeling came over me. The entire scenery didn't look, nor feel right. Once fully on the street I let the car falls to a slow creep. As I took in my surroundings, my phone rang, scaring the shit out of me.

"Yeah!" I answered.

"Is that you driving slow down the street?" Don asked.

"Yeah, where you at?"

"Stop right there I'm coming out."

"Alright." I double-park and waited. Soon, Don emerged from the cut carrying a brown paper bag and a book bag while holding his waist. As he made it to the street a car slowly rode passed. Don Grilled the two occupants. When the car passed he stopped in the middle of the street and whipped out a Mac -12 from his waist. The car bent the corner and Don continued towards my car and hopped in. I grabbed the book bag as he sat.

"Damn, slim you whipping out in the middle of the street?" I tossed the bag onto his lap.

"Letting them bitch ass nigga know I ain't playing. This is my hood. I gotta to --- this shit down. Here you go." He tossed the paper bag to me containing the money. Just as he was preparing to go out, I saw two niggas in all black emerge from the Alleyway.

"S, get down," Just as we ducked down the assault began. (BOC, BOC, BOC, BOC!)

"Pull off, pull off." Don yelled without lifting my head I put the car in drive and slammed the gas. The car took off destroying a few parked cars rearview mirrors. Cautiously, I sat up in time to make the left turn onto 13th.

"Circle back around." Don ordered. We circled the block. Once around front Don Men were out there. Don stepped out to holla at them, leaving his drugs and the Mac-12 behind. Just then, an unmarked police car pulled behind me. Behind it sat a jump out cruiser unleashing five undercover officers on Don and his crew. Without a second thought, they all ran. Trying to be as unobtrusive as possible, I attempted to pull off. *Whoop. Whoop*

"Turn your vehicle off" the officer yelled over the loud speaker. That was all the initiative I need to mash the Gas and sampled them people. I made the same left onto 13th street. It was just my luck that I ended up bumper to bumper with a squad car. I threw my car into reverse, but the unmarked was on my ass. They had me sandwiched. I gripped the Glock on my lap with thoughts of holding court in the streets. One of my biggest fears was dying by the hands of another. That thought easily remained just that. *A thought.*

"Fuck!" I yelled out in frustration. I placed my Glock on the dash and slowly extended my hands out the window. Officers quickly surrounding the car with their guns drawn. I was snatched out and slammed down where I was cuffed and placed in a transport cruiser. It was there that I lowered my head in defeat as I was catered off to the Third District Police Station.

Once there, I sat in the interrogation room with my head in disarray. I knew I should not have gone against my better judgment. I had to get in contact with Ashley. I pray she could make this go away. Some men were built for jail; I didn't consider myself one of those people. It was about an hour later before the detective finally walked in. the detective was a fat white man who looked like he had a sweating problem. As he sat down, he wiped his brow with a handkerchief, and placed a small folder on the table.

Charles Black, 716 and Kennedy St. First thing that I want to know is how is it that you have so much drugs, and two guns, and I don't know who the hell you are? Records clean. My guess is, you've been doing something right for a long time. Then I see Donald Dyson, AKA Don, a known criminal of the highest street caliber and on my most wanted list, jump out of your car moments after multiple gunshots are heard in the area. Do you know what that's tells my Mr.

Black? It tells me that you have to be just as big a criminal as he is. Now as for you, you don't have a record so you're looking at about 15 years minimum. Got anything you want to tell me about the guns and drugs that were found in your car?" He closed the folder and leaned back in his chair.

"I ain't talking to you about shit let me get my phone call." I stood my ground.

"Suit yourself. Can't say that I didn't try to help you." Det. Pike stood and walked out. Seconds later a female brought me the phone. As quick as I could I called Ashley. Both Marcus and I, knew Ashley since we were kids. Just so happened when Marcus went to jail Ashley and I began a blossoming relationship. She grew up with aspirations to one-day join the FBI so she became a police officer for the Third District Metropolitan Police Department. I knew that if anyone could get me out of this mess, she could.

"Hello." Her angelic voice answered

"Ashley, I'm in trouble and I desperately need your help."

"Chucky, why are you calling me from a number in 3rd District?" I could hear the worry in her voice.

"I'm locked up, Ash."

"You stupid motherfucker! I told you. I told your stupid ass to slow down. Now look at you." She was pissed and nothing short if how I knew she would be.

"Calm down Ashley, you can chew me out when I get home. Right now, I need you to make this shit go away."

"And how the fuck am I supposed to do that?"

"I don't know, you the fucking police. Figure it out." I was becoming irritated from her lack of.

"What did you get caught with?"

"A quarter brick, and a pound of Loud and two guns."

"You are a stupid ass, Chucky. Who's the arresting officer?"

"Det. Pike!"

"Shit, that motherfucker is a straight up cop. This isn't going to be easy Chucky, and I know he's gonna want something in return for making the shit disappear."

"No promises Chucky, I'll see what I can do."

"Aright, baby girl, I love you."

"Kiss my ass Chucky." She hung up.

-Ashley-

Time after time again, I warned Chucky that if he didn't slow down that his wrongs would catch up to him. Now it has, he expected me to make this go away. I had no leverage to do that. Det. Pike was a hard nose cop and strictly by the book. Plus, I don't think he liked me too much; from when he tried to take me out to dinner and I declined his offer.

To win him over would be a task. I started to call Det. Pike, but thought better of it, thinking this was something that needed to be done face to face. I made my way inside with my eyes searching for Pike. They eventually locked on him at his desk.

"Bingo!" I said to myself and made my way over.

"Morning, Pike." I greeted. He looked up and smiled.

Ahh, the beautiful Ms. Ashley Robinson. Officer, that is. How may I help out?" Det. Pike leaned back interlocking his fingers behind his head.

"You locked up a Charles Black tonight." I got straight to it.

"Yep, sure did. What about him?" He sat forward almost showing his fangs.

"I need a favor."

"I don't do favors, but what is it."

"I need you to drop the case and I owe you one." I sated. Det. Pike laughed.

"You, of all people should know that ain't gonna happen."

"Well then he'll pay you to drop it." I pushed.

"Careful there officer, bribing a decorated officer won't look good on your resume." He sarcastically smiled.

"Come on Pike, do this to me. Please I'll owe you big time."

"You must really care about this scumbag, huh?" he asked.

"Yes, I do. I personally don't think he'll make it a week over D.C Jail. Please Pike I'll do anything." With my words and the look on Det. Pike face. I knew that I'd made a mistake.

"Anything, you say?" Det. Pike smiled like The Grinch Who Stole Christmas.

"Yes!" I looked to the ground knowing where this conversation was headed.

"You know what Officer Ashley? Can I call you Officer Ashley? He stood up and stepped towards me. He was so close I could smell the Camel cigarettes that he smoked. "Ill make this whole thing go away. It will be all for you, but I will need 21 favors from you.

"Stop beating around the bush, Pike." I showed my impatience.

"Beating around the bush is the last thing that I want to do. Bad choice of words, I want to tast the bush, and then beat the bush Officer Ashley. Twenty-one encounters on my time. when I want it, where I want it. How I want it. I've been wanting a shot of your pussy for a long time now, so if you want your little boyfriend off the hook..." He grabbed my pussy. "You're gonna give me everything that your body has to offer. Do we have a deal?" Knowing what I had to do, I thought of how much I loved Chucky. The love I held for him was unconditional. Therefore, if I had to set out some ass to this sweaty motherfucker to get my man home them so be it.

"It's a deal. When will he be released?"

"That's not all Officer Ashley. Let him know that he has to give me a murder that is worth something. A murder that's cut a dry. If I don't get my murder, then all bets are off. Moreover, I'm locking your ass up for Bribery. You can leave my office now, and I'll be in touch." Just as I turned to leave, Det. Pike slapped me on the ass.

"Keep it tight Officer." he smiled. I realized at that point that I had just made a deal with the devil. Now, not only was Chucky freedom on the line my career was also. After this, Chucky would have to leave the streets alone for good or he would lose me forever.

Chapter 5

-Marcus-

I opened my eyes to the sound of Chucky entering the apartment. I was so distraught about my encounter with my mother that I didn't even remember coming here. It didn't matter to me no way. All that mattered was the fact that I was neglected yet again by my mother. It hurt me even more just thinking how a mother could not love her only son who in turn loved her unconditionally.

I sat up resting my elbows on my knees with my forehead in my palms. My head thumped with aggression. I could smell perfume on me, and thought that maybe it was my mother's when I hugged her.

"I see you finally got up. Where did you go last night?" Chucky inquired.

"I stepped out to smoke a cigarette." I said as I wiped Cole out of my eye. My mood was somber and Chucky could tell. Come on Marcus you can't let your mom tear you down. Let it make you stronger, slim." Chucky sat next to me. I saw now as good as anytime to ask what's been weighing on my mind.

"What do you want for me Chucky? Why are you so hell bent on helping me? My own mother wouldn't do that. What's your motive; because how I see it everyone got one.

"My motive?" Chucky repeated in disbelief.

"Yeah, your motive." I Spoke in a serious tone.

"Nigga, my motive is that I'm your friend, and not gonna see you do bad. If I'm wrong for that, I don't want to be right." Chucky laid it on. I stood and grabbed my property bag from Oak hill. I opened it and easily found what I was looking for.

"Aright, you want to help then help me find them." I handed Chucky a piece of paper with the names Thomas Kennedy, and Terrica Barr etched on it.

"These are the names of the lawyer, and the advocate." Chucky looked to me for clarification.

"Yeah, They're both gonna pay for what they did to me. I waited seven years to get next to them. Now, I am home. I'm gonna be sure to do just that.

"So what do you need from me?" Chucky tossed the paper on the table.

"Just help me find them and I'll take it from there." I could tell that Chucky was reluctantly hesitant to help me. For a few minutes, he sat there looking into space. I guess he was weighing his loyalty to his freedom.

"You sure you want to do this?" He asked.

"The question is, are YOU sure you want to do this? You told me when I was in Oak hill that you would help me do whatever I wanted. This is what I want. Once I start, there is no turning back. If you ain't with it then I'd advise you to steer clear." I wanted. I also made my mind up that if rolled with me and chocked I'd kill him."

"Good! Now find out where them people at and I'll take it from there." I then made my way to the bathroom. Once inside, I realized I didn't have a toothbrush or washcloth. I turned to ask Chucky for some assistance, but he was right there.

"Here go some hygiene shit I picked up for you. Just grab a towel off the rack." Chucky pointed.

"Thanks." I replied and closed the door. Inside, I thought of the keen presentation I put on. Truthfully, I wondered myself if I could carry out the task of taking another's life. Thinking, how I would react once I was placed in that position. I guess it would be answered in due time.

I turned the showerhead to full blast with hot water. It was the only thing I could think of to erase the smell of Oak hill from my body. I let the water bead down on my head excepting every ounce of pain applied to my skin. Guess you could say I was trying to burn away the mental anguish I was experiencing.

I turned the water off a little too soon, but knew I had to get out in order to cease the day with all of my aspirations.

As I stepped out and began to towel off a thought arose in my mind. Clothes! As if on cue, Chucky knocked on the door.

"Marcus I got some clothes for you."

"Thanks, Chuck." I opened the door and grabbed them.

"No problem! I'm about to cook us something to eat so hurry up."

"Aright, I'm getting dressed right now." I replied through the door. Once dressed, I looked at myself in the, mirror. I truly enjoyed the sight, but it didn't mean anything when you didn't have a dime in your pocket. A part of my mind half expected to see Chucky at the door holding a wad of money, but that didn't happen. I stepped out following my nose to the smells of breakfast. I stepped in the kitchen and chose a random seat. Chucky stood at the stove with his back turned.

"I know I asked you this already, but what are you doing for money?" Chucky asked without turning around.

"Whatever you have in mind. I'm just really trying to keep my head above water, until I handle my business. After that I will focus on stacking some money." I replied. Chucky turned around.

"Well I got a gallon of PCP for you. I'll help you get I off, but if you fuck that money up you're on your own. As far as them people on that list I'm here for you no matter what. We just gotta make sure that we do it the right way. I can't do jail so we got to be careful. I got a lot of love for you slim and want to see you exact your revenue properly. From now on we're a team, so when you move hip me to what's up and I'll do the same. Lastly, but not least. If we get knocked and end up in jail behind this, we keep out mouths shut. Period! Are we understood?" Chucky's eyes became a most serious glare.

"Over stood, but getting caught not an option. Especially, before that list complete. If I get knocked before the list is complete then so be it. I'll eat my time, but my first thought is kill and not be caught." I paused, and then looked Chucky in the eye. "You know you don't have to help me do this." I stated because I wasn't sure if he had ever done anything like this before.

"I know that, but it's my loyalty to you and this street shit that won't let me do otherwise. My decision is made, so let's get started and end this in the first quarter.

"Say no more." I replied. Chucky seemed so sure about his intentions, and carrying them out. I kind of felt bad because although I spoke a good game, I was.

"Hello!" She answered.

"What's up Ash?" I greeted.

"Why the fuck you took so long to call me. You wouldn't be out there if it wasn't for me." She yelled.

"Aight, I'm calling you now. So what's up how did you do it?" I looked at Marcus to see if he was tuned in to our conversation, but he gave no signs to confirm that.

"He said that you would have to give him a murder that's worth something. If you don't, then he's going to lock me up for attempting to bribe an officer. I can't believe that you got me caught up in this bullshit."

"So where do you stand with this. What do you want me to do?" I asked not sure of her intentions.

"Fuck do you mean, where do I stand? You're gonna give me what he want and I'll take care of my end."

"So he wants something that's worth something, huh?" The thought spun in my mind.

"Yeah, so will you do it or what, do I have to have him lock your stupid ass up. I'm losing my entire career because of your pride. So what's up?" Ashley was putting the full court press on me. As the conversation him preceded, I eyed Marcus list and decided that God placed my get out of jail free card in the chair across from me.

"Come on Chucky you know the circumstances of my life. Do I have to answer that?" I asked feeling a little ashamed and embarrassed at my lack of sexual experience.

"Alright, alright we gonna see if we can fix that then. It's impossible to be around me and be a virgin." Chucky slightly laughed. I could tell that he was suppressing his laughter. My blood began to boil. I pulled out the nine and cocked it on the table. I then stared Chucky dead in his eyes.

"Chucky, let this be the last time you use my chaste and I as a center piece of something to amuse you." My face sat stone like. Expressionless, with the seriousness of the gun on the table. Barrel pointing at him. Chucky's smile and suppressed laughter vanished.

"That's not funny Marcus." Chucky replied in a frightened voice.

"Neither is my virginity. You have the slightest idea what I been through these last seven years? I refuse to let you sit here and make a joke out of the worst time of my life. Make that your last time. dig me!" I slated with more aggression then needed, but I wanted my point made.

"You got that Marcus. My apologies. Let's not let this dampen our relationship." Chucky insisted. Before I could reply, there was a knock on the door. I grabbed the nine and went to it. Chucky just looked on in amazement, but opted not to say anything. I gradually looked out the peephole instantly recognizing Ashley. I tucked the nine on my abdomen and opened the door.

"Marrrrccuuss!" Ashley screamed with excitement. She jumped in my arms with her legs wrapping around my waist. This was the first time that I had held a woman in such a manner. Just that simple act made my hormones churn harder. Once I put her down, she lifted my shirt exposing the butt of the gun.

"Marcus you haven't been home two days, and already have a gun on your waist." She stated and then looked at Chucky who raised his palms in a form of mock surrender.

"Don't look at me; he's his own man." Chucky smiled.

"Forget about that Ash, look at you though. All grown up, with a gun and a police uniform." I couldn't help but lust after Ashley and her long brown hair and creamy red complexion. Her uniform accented her every curve. I had the slightest idea of what to do with a woman of her caliber. Ashley stood there with her bottom lip poked out as if she were mad. I pulled her close for a hug and she smiled.

"I ain't forgetting about that gun big head, and I know you gave it to him Chucky. Don't make me lock your ass up." She stated sounding as serious as she could. Chucky's smile even disappeared. I guess he knew or felt that she was serious. I thought that I'd be nervous when dealing with a woman, but with Ashley it was different. Everything was natural and felt genuine. Both coming and going.

"Marcus, you've been away now for seven years with no childhood what do you plan on doing now that you're home." She looked in my eyes silently telling me that she wanted a truthful answer.

"Live my life. What else is there to do?"

"Don't get smart boy, you know what I mean." She nudged my head.

"First I have a few people I need to see. Then I'm gonna work on me" I looked at Chucky.

"Well don't let Chucky influence you to do the wrong thing. Right now, because of his drug dealing ways, his future lay in the hands of another." Ashley looked to Chucky with scolding eyes.

"I'm not understanding what you're saying." I informed because I remember Chucky saying I've never been locked up!

"Probation!" Chucky blurted out before Ashley could reply.

"Chucky caught a drug charge after I told him he was being watched. Hard head make a soft ass and he learned the hard way." Ashley explained. I wondered why Chucky would lie to me.

"And I got probation, so what's the big deal. It's over now." I could tell that this was a conversation that Chucky was not trying to have.

"Over my ass. The big deal is that you need to get your life together, and it's not over until you finish the terms of your probation, so don't get lax." Ashley scolded like a mother to child. Listening to them converse I got the feeling that there was more behind their words then the face value. Then I wondered had Chucky ever been intimate with Ashley as an adult? Still, we conversed remembering our short lived past.

➤ Schizophrenia

62

Chapter 6

-Marcus-

It was about 7:15 am in the morning. I'd been home now for three days and was on the apartments front eating breakfast from a carry out called wings and things. As I ate, my eyes stayed glued to my mother's house. I was impatiently waiting for her to emerge. Even though she professed how much she hated me I still saw her as my mother and loved her as such.

Around 7:30 am, my mother's front door swung open with her stepping out wearing an all-white nurse uniform. I thought she looked so beautiful. By the time she made it to the middle of the steps, I guess it was her motherly instincts that caused her to look up. Everything stood still and fell silent as we locked eyes. Suddenly, she took off running towards her truck.

"Ma wait!" I hopped up from the steps with my food hitting the ground. I took off into a mad sprint desperately trying to catch my feeing mother. She hopped in her truck as I was quickly approaching. Just as I reached the back of the truck, the tire screeched off gliding the SUV up the street. Again, I was so close yet so far away. Rejection was yet again staring me in the face.

I walked towards Chucky's building occasionally looking back hopping to see her returning for me. Hope was lost and I ended up back on Chucky's front. I picked up my soiled food and returned back to the apartment. Inside, Chucky was up and at the computer.

"I'm glad you're in. come here, I want you to look at this." Chucky pointed at the screen. I walked over, still in a somber mood. That being, I said nothing and allowed Chucky to lead the conversation.

"Times have changed since you've been gone. Technology has become everything. They have a search engine called FACEBOOK that everybody and their mother is apart of. If you want to find anyone in the U.S. there's a 90% change that their on there."

"So you think the names on my list are on there?" I asked for my own comprehension.

"It's a good chance that they are. If not, then its going to be a lot harder to find them"

"Well type in Thomas Kennedy. That was my lawyer." I instructed my heartbeat with anticipation awaiting confirmation as Chucky's fingers clicked away. It only took seconds for his request to go through. Either it was luck or just plain fate, but there were about 25 people with the name Thomas Kennedy. After scanning each name my eyes landed on Thomas Kennedy Esq. The Esq. meant Esquire. In laymen terms, LAWYER!

"Click on the one that say Esq." I pointed and Chucky complied. By Chucky's double click the screen changed, now revealing what looked to be a website for a law firm called Kennedy and Lotz. I grabbed a piece of paper and wrote down the address.

"Is that him?" Chucky asked just as he found a picture of the man.

"Without question." I said in almost a whisper. My blood began to boil by the sight of him. I was positive it was him. He was one of two faces engraved into my mind as if it were done by a chisel and hammer.

"It's still early, you want to get him tonight?" Chucky looked at me with an optimistic glare.

"Naw, I want to go see him in person first. Like you said, we gotta do this the right way. The time will present itself." I started walking towards the back.

"How do you plan on seeing him in person?" Chucky yelled to my back.

"How else? Walk straight in his office." I yelled over my shoulder and closed the door. I left Chucky in the company of his own thoughts.

-Marcus-

After taking a shower, it was about 8:30 am. My mind was no longer on my mother's neglect, but solely on seeing Mr. Kennedy with my own eyes. I stood in front of a full body mirror straightening my tie. To someone on the outside of the square, one would think I was lawyer myself. My crisp oxford shirt and gold cuff plated cufflinks I was truly in a realm that was foreign. My business attire was all due to Chucky. I knew that Chucky may have had my best interest at heart, but with him already lying to me was making it a little harder to fully trust him.

The weather was pretty hot, so I opted not to adorn the blazer that went with my attire. I grabbed Chucky leather briefcase and was out. As I walked passed the living room Chucky still sat at the computer. Seeing me within his peripheral, he looked up.

"Where are you headed?" He non-chalantly questioned.

"To the Law Offices of Kennedy and Lotz." I replied and grabbed Chucky's car keys from the table.

"So you're going to just walk in there, kill the man and walk out? And who said you could take my car?" Chucky doubled up his questioning. Unbeknownst aiding my suspensions.

"Be smarter than that Chucky. I'm just going to get a visual on my target. Be back in couple of hours. And you said I could take your car because you didn't know that I couldn't." I began making my way to the door.

"You sure you're ready to drive?" chucky sounded concerned.

"This is the best time as any to learn. See you in a couple." With that said I was out the door ready to face my first conquest head on. Stepping back outside I couldn't help but look back to my mother's house. I was hard, but I fought to suppress the tears welling up behind my eyes. My mother was a topic that I felt I would never come to grips with. Basically, it was a delicate matter.

I made it to the front of the BMW. Facing it, like a formidable adversary preparing for battle. My task was to conquer the automobile and use it how I saw it. Gaining my courage, I stepped to the driver's side unlocking the locks and taking a seat atop of the peanut butter rich leathers.

I wrapped my fingers around the leather laced stirring wheel, and took a deep breath thinking, I can do this. Turning the ignition, I brought the machine to life. The stereo blared the sounds of Tupac's Hit'em up.

After turning it down, and hitting the gas the engine purred. I placed the car in drive allowing it to roll out of its parking space. As I pulled into traffic, sporadically I would tap the gas. Slowly, the task became natural to me. Before long, I was pulling up to the building of Kennedy, Lotz and Associates.

On sight of the name, my stomach became nauseous. I was nervous. Again, I questioned if I'd be able to do this? Could I become that same killer I was when I was twelve? That couldn't be answered until Thomas Kennedy was staring down the barrel of my gun.

Finding a parking space on Indiana Ave was hell in itself. I circled various blocks for fifteen minutes before I finally found one about a block and a half away. Walking back, the butterflies in my stomach overwhelmed me with each step. So much so that at times I'd have to stop to gather my barrens. Once back in front of the building I took a deep breath and proceeded with my plans of revenge.

Stepping inside, I was greeted by a 48x40 inch portrait of Kennedy and his associates. The motherfucker hadn't aged a bit. I would never forget his face. The sight of it made my blood boil. My eyes were fixated on this still portrait that I never noticed Kennedy's secretary eyes burning a hole through me.

"Change occurs with everything, but that portrait will not. Can I help you sir?" The old woman asked with a slight attitude. She reminded me of Aunt Bee from the old sitcom The Andy Griffith show. Her sudden statement slightly baffled me. I caught my words in my throat. I knew that if didn't speak quick that she'd notice my nervousness. From out of my peripheral, I was a door open. Without a care in the world out walz Thomas Kennedy. Without giving me so much as the slightest eye contact, he began to speak with the receptionist.

"Roberts, I want you to cancel all of my appointments for the rest of the day and re-schedule them. I have a few loose ends I need to take care of before the banquette tonight."

"Will do sir, did you ever find a spot to have it at?" She asked.

"Yeah, but it took some doing. I managed to secure a master ballroom at the Holiday Inn in Silver Spring. Everything starts at seven, so be there or be square. Also call Sir Williams Florist on 14th street and have them deliver a dozen roses to my wife at the house." Kennedy smiled, tossed his keys in the air and caught them in his palm. Still, he paid me no mind as if I weren't there. It took everything within me not to exact my revenge on the spot. I knew I had to be smart so I allowed him to walk right passed me. As he did, my eyes shot daggers at him. For a second, I forgot where I was until the receptionist spoke.

"Sir, can I please help you?" She spoke again now clearly frustrated.

"Not at all." I replied. Cobweb housing bitch! I mumbled to myself. Not once taking my eyes off Kennedy's back. I stepped out of the firm in hot pursuit. Once outside, I was stopped.

"Marcus!" A female voice called out to me. I turned to see Ashley jogging towards me. My eyes immediately began to lust over her womanly curves gripped tightly by her sky-blue spandex. Seeing her reminded me that I had yet to have sex. More importantly, that I was down town in broad daylight.

"You're the last person that I expected to see down here. What's going on?" She hugged me sensually pressing her body against mines. I instantly gained an erection.

"Just trying to find some type of work. Not trying to do anything to make you lock me up." I smiled as the lie rolled of my tongue.

"Well I'm glad to hear that, but something tells me that you will, and need me to get you out. Chucky is hardheaded. I don't want to see you end up like him."

"I'm good, Chucky and I are two totally different people." I assured.

"Yeah, we'll see." She replied as if the thought saddened her. I pulled her close. She didn't resist and laid her head on my shoulder.

"So what's up with you, I see you keeping that physique right." I released her to take in her entire body.

"I went thought the Academy's basic training so I had to stay in shape. When it was over, I just stuck with it. I scored so high on the written I was offered a job with the DEA, so I took it. Watching Chucky do the things that he does, goes against my entire oath as an officer.

"You got to separate the ones you love from your job." We locked eyes causing a brief silence before I broke it.

"So where is the lucky man in your life?" I shot. The question caught her off guard by her hesitation.

"Well, well just say that he's on thin ice as we speak."

"Is there any room for you to meet new friends?" Again, we locked eyes.

"No!....." She said a little too quick." I mean no, there's no room to meet new friends…" I was crushed. "But there's always room for old ones." She continued. At first, I didn't know it, but I was smiling from ear to ear. So was she. At that moment, an awkward silence arose along with the intensity of our peeking sexual hunger for one another. Something was pulling us towards each other our lips met igniting a flame that was dying to burn between us. Her lips tasted like honey straight off the comb. Just as I pulled her close with her breast pressed to my chest, she pulled away.

"I'm… I'm sorry Marcus. I, I, I didn't mean to…" I cut her off.

"It's cool, I enjoyed it." I smiled to lighten the moment.

"Me too!" She smiled through her sudden coyness like a schoolgirl. "I have Marcus. I guess I'll be seeing you around." Her voice was beautiful I thought to myself.

"I hope so." I touched my lips savoring the moment. Ashley stood on her tippy toes giving me a peck on the cheek. She smiled again, and then continued her stride never once looking back. My eyes remained glued to her backside as all kinds of sexual acts flooded my mind. Once she was out of sight my eyes fell to the large gold sign of Kennedy and Lotz, then I thought to myself. "Out of sight, out of mind."

"I haven't seen Marcus in over seven long years.. even then, we weren't boyfriend and girlfriend. I will admit though that I had the biggest crush on him. So much so that back then I was scared to even talk to him. That was my reasoning behind telling Chucky to bring him over ny house the day he went away. Chucky was there, when Marcus wasn't. I guess that is why I fell in love with him. Now, with Marcus being home, I was now questioning the validity of the love that I thought I had for Chucky. At this point, I was confused and did not know what to feel.

After usual five-mile run, I made it home exhausted. My legs burned and my lime green spandex shorts were drenched in my sweat. I kicked off my shoes and socks and made my way to the bathroom to run a bath. After my run, I needed to relax my muscles. As I poured the Herbal Essence Bubble Bath, I bent over to check the waters temperature.

"Now that's a sight that a sane man can never forget." A deep voice resounded from the door, naturally starling me, I turned around holding my chest to see that it was Det. Pike.

"How the fuck did you get in my house?" I was at a lost for words.

"Now is that any way to treat a guess?" He stepped in the bathroom.

"You can wait in the living room. I have to get dressed. Afterwards we can talk about our arrangement." My body quivered as this fat motherfucker towered over me.

"Oh noo, Officer Ashley. I want the bush wet and sweaty, and for the record, talking is the last thing that I came to do." He rubbed my check. I was concerned. He then leaned in with a white tongue and licked the sweat from my temple. With little effort, he placed his massive hands under my armpits and picked me up to sit me on the sink. Aggressively, he spread my thighs in one swift motion, then slowly stepped between them. He leaned in to the point of his nose touching mines.

"You don't know how much I'm going to enjoy this." His breath was hot and smelled of garlic. I said nothing and turned my head from the horrid smell. Forcefully, he pressed his lips against mines, kissing me long and hard. Det. Pike suddenly laughed and smiled one of greed and triumph. Pike looked in my eyes, and then slowly kneeled. He put his nose to my pussy and took a whiff of my pheromones. He drug his nasty white tongue from my pussy, outside of my shorts to my navel then to my mouth. As his tongue entered and found mines, I almost spit up. His hands came to life as he grabbed two handfuls of my shorts pulling them down my sweaty thighs. He looked down to my bald pussy lips.

"No bush!" He looked in amazement. "And a butterfly." He smiled looking at me and back to my mound.

"Get what you came here for Pike." I spoke in almost a whisper, as I looked off not wanting to see my reality. tear fighting to explode behind my eyes.

"Trust and believe, I'm not going nowhere until I do, Officer Ashley." He smiled and undid his belt from his overlapping stomach. I anticipated the sight of what would be my sexual oppressor. Det. Pike dropped his pants revealing a semi- upward penis that hung a little past mid-thigh. He saw all the awe in my face as he began to stroke himself. A sight I didn't want him to notice. All the while holding a smile of arrogance.

"You're going to enjoy every inch of this, Officer Ashley. It's been a while since you had a dick this big. I can tell by how you're drooling over it. Don't worry though, you're gonna get every inch of this." As much as I hated to say it, with a dick as big as Pike's I was scared that he would have no regard for my insides. Det. Pike stepped back between my legs and slowly kneeled. He began to suck on my clit. His sandpaper like tongue flicked back and forth. When I looked, he had half of his face buried in my pussy. The roughness of his tongue caused extra stimulation that I wasn't expecting.

"Oh God!" I short moan escaped my lips before my mind could protest. I knew that Det. Pike had to have heard it because directly after, it was as if he was encouraged. He used his massive index finger working it in and out of my pussy as he devoured my clit. Then as if they had a mind of their own, my legs spread wider. My hand, moving behind Det. Pike's head. He was taking me to a place I didn't think he was capable of.

"Oh God, oh God I'm about to cum." Again, I moaned in pleasure. Det. Pike inserted two fingers sending me over the edge. "Oh God I'm cumming." My legs trembled as I leaned back on the mirror. He grabbed my knees pushing them further apart slurping up every drop of cum that my pussy shot out. Once he released my legs, he stood with that same arrogant smile of triumphant. He was the conquer, and I was the conquest. My head leaned against the wall as I waited for my breaths to even out.

"You look drained and pleased Officer Ashley." He stroked his dick that was now hardening to the occasion. Its length parallel to a child's forearm and scary in the least.

"Fuck you Pike!" I managed to assert between breaths.

"No Officer Ashley, I'm fucking you." He aimed his massive penis towards my pussy and cupped both of my ass cheeks in his large hands. He pulled me to the edge of the sink plunging his dick inside my cum drench walls. I could do nothing but Inhale a breath of air as I took every inch he gave. Simultaneously, Pike fucked me relentlessly before my legs wrapped around his waist with my arms around his neck. Before long, I was throwing my pussy back at him. We gained a rhythm that drew us both to near climax. Det. Pike pace began to quicken, followed by grunts and moans. His hands squeezed my ass tighter.. I could feel the head of his penis begin to swell inside of me. I was so caught up in gaining another orgasm myself that I disregarded his lack of a condom.

"I'm cumming again. OHHH God I'm cumming again!" I yelled. Det. Pike then exploded a load so big that it cascaded down my thighs. He pulled out and wiped his dick of with a washcloth. The whole while he smiled that same smile as before. Triumph! Without so much as one word to me, he dressed and just before he left he stopped at the threshold.

"Oh yeah, your boy hasn't gotten at me yet. time is ticking so get on your job." I said nothing in return, and watched the devil leave my house. standing on wobbly legs, I fell to the floor. Casually, I looked to my chest and saw a burgundy hicky.

"Shit!" I thought to myself.

Chapter 7

-Marcus-

The Holiday Inn in Silver Spring kept repeating itself in my mind. It took everything I had in me not to kill him where he stood. I had to realize, that at that precise moment there were so many variables that ended with me in jail. There were entirely too many people in a heavily police populated area. Kennedy, Lotz and Associates sat in the heart of the Court District where almost every police faction frequented.

The Holiday Inn was a priority but even still it was second option, and second to a last resort. How I saw it was if Sir Williams Florist was sending flowers to Kennedy wife then I'd bet my life they'd have an address for his home. If so, then this would be easier than expected. I shook loose the thought of Ashley and made my way home. Objectives: Get and Address for Sir Williams Florist.

Since I lost my food chasing my mother this morning I was dead hungry. While driving up Georgia Ave, I spotted a carry out called Fish In the Hood. I figured that it had to be good, so I pulled over and made my way inside. Upon entrance, a beautiful brown skin woman with a big ass that reminded me of Ashley captivated my eyes. I had not tried to court a woman since I had been home and even now I stood nervous. Suddenly, she looked back and caught me staring.

"Excuse me, are you gonna speak or just look at my ass?" She was bold I thought.

"My apologies Ma'am, I been locked up seven years. You're the thickest and prettiest woman I've seen in a long time. "She looked at me like she heard it all before.

"Yeah well it's not nice to stare. What's your name anyway?" She continued.

"Marcus and you?" She was making this easy.

"My name is Amanda. I'm from around Garfield." She replied.

"I'm from KDY." (Kennedy St.)

"Here you go ma'am that will be $10.85." The Chinese cashier stated Amanda began to reach in her purse. I placed a hand atop of hers.

"Keep your money, shawty. I got you." I looked to the cashier. "Put her bill on mines and give me six wings and fried rice and a extra large Ice Tea. I Placed a twenty in the booth and pulled my attention back to Amanda.

"You didn't have to do that I have my own money."

"I know that, but that don't mean that you have to use it. A man take care of his woman." I smiled with assurance.

"Who said I was your woman?" She smiled.

"Who said you wasn't She Matched my glare.

"Why don't you call me and find out exactly what I am." She stepped closer as if she was up for a challenge. She then unsnapped my phone from my hip and dialed her number. In turn I could hear her phone begin to ring in her purse. "You got my number so don't be afraid to use it. "She kissed her two fingers and touched my lips. I was wide open. She was aggressive, but a dish that I must have I got my food and headed home.

It took no time to get back to Kennedy Street. It was just straight shot back up Georgia Ave. when I pulled onto the street, I saw my mother in the hood of her truck. Quickly, I pulled in front of her and parked. At that point, I was thankful for the limo tints on Chucky's car. I parked with outdrawing any inferences from her. I stepped out and eased up behind her.

"Can I help you with that mother?" I asked seeing that she was only adding oil. My voice caused her to jump in short freight. When she turned, I saw nothing but discuss.

"No! I don't need anything from you. You've given me enough." Karen replied slamming the hood. She walked around to the driver's side of her truck. Just as she opened it, I slammed it shut.

"What do you mean, gave you enough?" I was clueless as to what she was talking. Whatever it was, I figured that it was the source of her hatred.

"Think about it Marcus, you've always been smart enough. Just think about it. I could see the tears welling up behind her eyes. She opened the door and hopped in. I was stuck, unable to move. Although my body was stick, my mind was moving a thousand miles a minute. Watching her pull off made me kill myself inside, because no matter how smart she said or thought that I was, I had no idea what it was that I gave her enough of.

"A Marcus!" I heard a voice yell. I turned to see Chucky on the buildings front. I turned back in time to see my mother's taillights bend the corner. I took a deep sigh and proceeded to where Chucky was.

"What's up Chucky>" I asked I approached the buildings steps.

"How did everything go at the law firm?" Chucky held the door open for me.

"I said that I was just going to look. Was that supposed to go a certain way?" I replied without giving him so much as a second glance as I walked pass.

"Whoa, Marcus I was just asking. Don't bite my head off." He spoke to my back. Stepping into the apartment, I began shedding the suit that I wore. Once I was in some more comfortable attire I went straight to the computer and booted up America online.

"So what happened, did you see him?" Chucky hovered over top of me as if he demanded an answer. From a child, My eyes instantly turned blood shot at the imprudence of him. I stood straight up easily towering over and looking down into his eyes.

"Look slim, stop asking me so many fucking questions. You asked and I answered. Let me handled my business. You dig where I'm at?" I swelled up for emphasis.

"Man, nigga ease up. I'm in this as much as you are." He replied in a feeling attempt to match my aggression.

"You ain't in shit. My business is my business. No witness, No Co-D dead body. Meaning, no one live to talk about it, but me. So if you with something. I hope you picked out a casket." Easing up I sat back down at the computer trying to mimic what I saw Chucky do once before.

"If you need anything, just know I got you. Damn!" Seeing that Chucky was adamant about helping me, I stopped trying and looked up at him.

"Well sit right here and find me an address for Sir Williams Florist." I smiled as sarcastically, as I could. Chucky seeing the minute task and took a seat at the screen. With a few short strokes of the keys, the website plastered its site on the screen. In bold yellow cursive lettering read the name of the Sir Williams Florist. I quickly jotted down the address and hours of operation and went to the back room shutting the door behind me. Naturally, I knew that I left Chucky dumbfounded. I hurried and dressed in to some street clothes then re-emerged. As I stepped out Chucky stood there obviously wanting answers like a hustler's bitch when her man was leaving in the middle of the night.

"You gonna tell me what's up?" Chucky folded his arms.

"Look slim, there's a banquette tonight at seven at the Holiday Inn in Silver Spring. I'm planning to catch Kennedy there." I straight faced lied. "Right now I'm going to the florist to get my mother some flowers sent to her house. I will be back around five."

"Aight, I take it this hit will require me to were a tuxedo?" Chucky questioned.

"More than likely," I replied.

"Aight, I'll take care of that this morning. I'm going to need your help tomorrow night as well. I have a big drop off to make to some guys I really don't like, but love their money. Just come and be my eyes and gun if need be." Chucky enlightened.

"Not a problem, I'll see you tonight." I replied without giving Chucky a chance to reply. I was out the door in a flash. I felt that it was imperative that I lie to Chucky. He was far too inquisitive for my liking. I would hate to kill him for asking one too many questions.

-Ashley-

I never thought that when Det. Pike left my house that my pussy would be so satisfied. Something that I didn't get on a rare basis. Det. Pike christened my pussy to a tee. It was to the point where I was looking forward to the next time he popped up in my house unannounced. Even though Det. Pike handled my pussy, as I've been needing, it was his hairy back, sweaty skin, and pungent stench of must, cigarettes and garlic breath. All making me feel dirty from the inside out.

Afterwards, I sat in the tub with vinegar and Epsom-salt in the water. I scrubbed my body until my skin turned red. Although I was willing, and actually enjoyed it, I still felt as if my womanhood was taken. As I scrubbed, I wondered why chucky had not called Det. Pike. He should have at least conferred with him. I grabbed the cordless and called him.

"Yeah!" He answered after about four rings.

"Why haven't you contacted, Det. Pike?" I was furious so I got straight to the point.

"Simple, I don't have his number. Second, I don't need you contacting me like this. Let ,me handle my business. I said I would handle it so let me do me."

"That's what the fuck I'm worried about. You doing you got us in this mess. Just get in contact with him, at least let him know that you're working on it. His number is 202 882 9923."

"Aight, everything goes right he might get the murder tonight." I was glad to hear that.

"Well keep your end and I'll keep my finger crossed." She urged, debating with herself whether or not to tell

Chucky about the other aspect of the agreement that she had to achieve.

"Alright bring your ass over here tonight around 11:00 pm."

"Okay, I'll see you then." Click! I hung up and leaned back into the water.

-Chucky-

I hung up the phone without a worry; since I knew Marcus plans for tonight. Had I not had this little bit of information Det. Pike would have been all over me. Now having Det. Pike phone number I felt that now was good a time as any to give him a call. Phase one in the fight for my life back and Marcus to lose his would manifest sooner than later. I picked up the cell phone and began dialing the numbers. It rung for about thirty seconds before someone answered.

"Det. Pike!" He answered in his usual husky voice.

"Pike this is Chucky." I waited for the name to register.

"Well if it isn't Mickey Mouse himself. Nice of you to check in. I hope you got something for me."

"Fuck you Pike you can cease the name calling. I'm still gangster ass nigga I was before this shit, so don't think that I won't touch your ass."

"You got a lot of balls Charles. I got your life in my right palm and your bitch pussy in the other. Now I don't think you want to lose both. After the good dicken I gave her earlier today she might be on my front porch with her tail waging and her tongue out." Det. Pike chuckled.

"What the fuck are you talking about?" I didn't believe him.

"Ask you bitch. Now, since we're passed the formalities give me my SHIT!" He demanded with no remorse for the latter.

"Nigga you lying. Ashley would never give your bad body ass no pussy."

"So you say. Then how do I know she keeps it bald with the tattoo of a butterfly on top. Now don't argue with me, Chucky. Talk to your bitch, until then tell me what the fuck I want know." I was vexed. I couldn't believe Ashley would do that to me.

"Look man, my targets name is Marcus Tidwell. He just got released from Oak hill a few days ago. He is planning to kill a lawyer named Thomas Kennedy. Kennedy was his juvenile lawyer. He tricked him into to signing a plea deal for Juvenile Life, while he was coerced to think that he would go home on the day that he was sentenced. He's planning to kill Kennedy at the Holiday Inn in Silver Spring, Maryland at seven tonight."

"I'm really starting to like you Chuck. You better not be spinning me, and remember your freedom is in my palm, and Ashley in the other. I'll be in touch." Click! He hung up.

Chapter 8

•————————•

-Marcus-

Closing the door to the beamer, I felt no indifference about feeding Chucky the half lies that I did. With the way that he's been acting coupled with him lying about being arrested I was beginning to get leery of him. I was beginning to regret telling him about my plans for revenge. I still saw him as a friend, but at times even friends could not be trusted.

I pulled up to Sir Williams Florist almost at a slow creep staring the structure down. After parking, I made my way inside. Stepping in, the air conditioning greeted my face with a cool welcome. The smell of flowers was euphoric. Easily, I became placed at ease. I looked toward the young girl behind the register and gave her a more then peaceful smile. That same smile became contagious as it found its way on her angelic face as well. she didn't look to be no older than 18 with blonde hair and blue eyes. Some would call her features the Typical American. As I approached the register, I could feel her eyes devouring my being.

"Excuse me ma'am, can you assist me please?" I asked politely.

"In more ways than one." She replied in a noticeably seductive tone, with a soft nibble on her bottom lip her boldness caught me off guard and I bashfully smiled. Staying focus, I foundated on the reason why I was there.

"Good, my father recently placed an order of flowers to be delivered to my mother. I would like to add to that order."

"What is your father name?" She asked with a hint of attitude. Once she noticed my blatant disregard of her advance.

"I think it may be under his company name. Kennedy, Lotz and Associates." How I saw it was if Kennedy Secretary placed the order than more than likely she billed it to the company. It was a long shot, but even a machine gun had a starting point before it hit its target.

"Yes, it's right here. The order was for two dozen roses going 6335 6th Northwest Washington D.C. What would you like to add to it?"

"In fact, on second thought. I'll just buy two dozen roses." I smiled again and just before the young girl followed suit. My guess was that she took my smile as a lusting manner. Little did she know my smile was of nothing but pure vengeance. Once I got the roses all I could think of was 6335 6th street. The first piece of my puzzle of revenge had been laid.

In an attempt to be as unobtrusive as possible, I knew I had to cover my tracks. Being so my next stop would be the Sunny Surplus. I was doing good staying focus on my task, but couldn't shake the feeling that I was being watched and followed. Cautiously, I looked through my mirrors but saw nothing that looked unusual. Maybe I was being paranoid. If I was, it was rightfully felt from what I was planning. Especially, if I wanted to kill and get away with it.

I knew that the key to getting away with it was not playing the part, but looking the part as well. at the Surplus, I bought a Navy Blue Dickle set and had a patch made that said Sir Williams Florist. To the naked eye, and the hope of just a glance I knew I could pass over. At least, I hoped I could pass over.

The street was located downtown in the Georgetown section of Washington D.C. It didn't take long to get there. After finding the address, I passed through once to get a look at the house. doing so, I noticed a Benz truck and a 750IL BMW in the driveway. I kept it moving, finding a secluded area to put on my makeshift uniform. With me placing the uniform on massive butterflies engulfed my stomach. My entire body shook with what felt like fear.

At that point, it confused me. How could I be fearful of anything when I was the one holding the gun? This was the day of reckoning. The day for settling all accounts. The day to be dauntless, even if never again.

I grabbed my nine making sure I had a full clip with one in the head. I tucked it on my waist just as perspiration began to form along my brow. I took a deep breath in a feeble attempt to calm myself. My nerves were shot to the point where it became a task in itself just to stand and walk.

With all the power in my body, I pushed one foot in front of the other. My heart resounded in my temple like an unforgiving migraine. My breath felt shortened. With every exhaled sigh. Constantly, I kept having to re-adjust the flowers in my hand from the sweat saturating my palms. Faster than I liked, I reached the house.

Standing on the porch, I marveled at the gold number 6335. I could hear the soft sounds of jazz pouring from behind the doors. I pressed the doorbell only to wait briefly. I could soon hear the heels of a woman clicking as she approached. If my nerves shot before, they were non-existent now. I easily realized that this might be something that I just could not do.

Pearl was different, he was hurting the woman who bore me. The woman who I held close and dear to my heart. I had come to grips that being a revenge stricken killer was just something that I wasn't. finally, without notice the door swung open revealing a beautiful bronze woman with shoulder length hair.

"May I help you sir?" She didn't bother looking at me from the hypnotization of the roses. It was the immediate anxiety that shook my body and soul to the core.

"Sorry, wrong address." Was all I could profess before I spun on my heels and made my way back down the driveway. I practically ran to the car felling as if I was having a borderline nervous breakdown. Once inside the car, I rested my head on the stirring wheel taking controlled breaths to calm myself. At that point, I could hear Marcell's words loud and clear. You ain't no killer. I'm the killer that you want to be. The reason you killed Pearl was because he was charging at you and you got scared. You a coward, Marcus. The kind of coward I despise, you scary motherfucker.

Those were the words of Marcell in one of our many conversations. Marcell always made a lot of sense. So much so, that he made me wonder if I really was a coward. He also talked a lot of bullshit too. He was a con's con artist with a helleva bluff game. Not to mention, he hated to be tested or his pride to be touched. Being so, and his self-proclaiming to be this cold hearted killer, I was going to see if he was about his work. I didn't want to involve a second party, but Kennedy had to die, and I just didn't have the courage to do it.

I lift my head from the stirring wheel and retrieved my cell phone. Scrolling through the phone book, I found Marcell number and pressed send. Shortly after, the phone began ringing. I hoped he'd answer this time. he never does, but now was of a detrimental nature. His answering machine picked up. Damn!

[You know who the fuck you called, leave a message. Peace bitches!]

After hearing this unruly prompt I left message.

"What's good Marcell? Okay you were right. I will admit you were right. I'm not the killer I thought that was. I couldn't, just like you said I couldn't we're past that now, but personally I don't think your half the killer you say you are. We know I'm not, but we don't know about you. I mean if you're any type of killer as you say you are, and so close to me than show me your that cold blooded killer that you say you are, and kill Kennedy. His address is 6335 6th street." I hung up. The bait was now set. I knew that if Marcell didn't kill Kennedy, then Kennedy just wouldn't die. His fate new rested in Marcell's hands. All I could do now was wait.

-Marcell-

I was sitting behind the wheel of my car in a deep yawn. My cell phone began vibrating. I looked at it seeing I had one new message. Looking at who sent it, I smiled. That smile grew as I listened to it.

So I was right. Marcus is a scary motherfucker. I kind of expected this text when I saw him run from Kennedy house. Bitch ass nigga. I thought. Then the message really hit me. Marcus thought I was bluffing. I wasn't bluffing about no part of my kill game, and had no problem showing him how a cold-blooded killer got down. In so many ways Marcus and I were just alike. Going hand in hand though, we were like night and day. Not a drop of blood in my body said Bitch! Or coward! Marcus was the epitome of it. I already knew Marcus couldn't do it. That's why I've been following his every move since Sir Williams Florist. I wanted to walk up the street to his car and scream on his bitch ass for even doubting me, but then I decided to let my actions speak than words ever could.

I checked my nine for a full clip and began making my way to the house. my heart rate was normal. This would be a walk in the park for me, unlike Marcus scary ass. I lived for this shit.

Soon the house came into my visual, enticing my hunger more and more with each step that I took. For Marcus, I would do this. I felt that we had a bond that a set of twins would have. He was like a brother to me. In turn, I would treat him as such.

I hoped the steps two at a time anxiously pressing the doorbell. Impatiently, I waited with my palms gripping the nine ever so elegantly. Hearing the clicking of heels approaching was like nails to a chalkboard. Finally, the clicking stopped and the front door swung open with a bronze colored woman holding her hand on her hip.

"So you did have the correct address." She said before looking to see who it was.

"Who said that we had it wrong the first time?" I replied before raising the nine to her face. With just a short twitch of my finger, I sent a bullet crashing through her forehead BOOM! The impact easily lift her off the ground and back into the foyer of her home. I stepped inside in full attack mode. In the near distance, I could hear a baby crying. My eyes searched for any movement in any direction. I turned into the living room to little girl looking to be no older than 13 years old. She sat terror stricken by seeing her mother's head turn the wooden floor crimson. The sight destroyed her conscious state. I stood over her as she sat on the couch. My nine smoking like a chimney on a winter's night and clutched tightly in my palm.

"Plc., Please don't hurt me. She looked up with watering eyes spread wide with fear. Surrender pouring from her pupils. I brought the gun up to my lips.

"Shhh, don't cry." As if on cue, the young girl released her tear ducts. Somehow and for some reason, this infuriated me. "I said don't cry." WACK! I sent the nine crashing down the side of her temple. Her body crumbled to the floor unconscious of the death that towered over her. With blatant and premeditated thought. I aimed at the girls head.

"Hey what the hell are you doing?" My attention fled from the young girl to the steps. I smiled a smile of destruction and mayhem.

Bingo! I thought. Low and behold, I was standing face to face with the man of the hour. Thomas Kennedy.

"Hey Tommy, I been looking for ya." My voice was cold and sinister. I took the crosshairs off the young girl and placed them on Kennedy. Kennedy continued down the steps not yet noticing his dead wife sprawled out at is feet. Reaching the bottom of the stairs and seeing the massive amount of blood his eyes finally fell to his wife's corpse. Instantly his legs fell languish as he dropped to his wife's side.

"Oh God, Stephanie, please God no! Kennedy brought his wife head to his lap. Tears streamed down his face. Slowly, as his anger consumed his eyes, they traveled along the floor and up my body until they looked on my own. The snarl on his face let me know that he wasn't too happy with me.

"You fucking murderer!" He yelled with driblets of saliva shooting from his mouth.

"Temper, temper Tommy. You shouldn't be insulting people that have a gun in his hand!" I yelled. Not to mention no regard for human life." I spoke calmly.

"You fucking basted. You killed my wife." Kennedy's chest rose with uncontrolled anger.

"You don't believe shit stink do you. Tommy?" Maybe this will help you. BOOM! Without taking my eyes off Kennedy I aimed to the floor releasing one bullet into the young girls head. Her body gave off a slight twitch before eternally lying still." Can you smell the shit yet Tommy?" I gave a slight chuckle. Holding his dead wife in his arms and seeing his oldest child be stripped of her life drained every ounce of his will to win, his will to live. Kennedy bowed his head in a short prayer, and used his thumb and index finger to close his wife's eyes.

Gently he laid her head down and slowly stood to his feet. Suddenly he took off running towards me like freight train. I waited till he got close enough then at the last second smashed the nine across his temple. Kennedy fell to my feet sobbing uncontrollably. Methodically, I moved to the side of him sending my boot crashing into his face. Dazed. Kennedy fell to his back and for the first time spoke submissively.

"You've gone and killed my whole family. What have I done so drastic to deserve this." Kennedy looked up with pleading eyes.

"Does the name Marcus Tidwell ring a bell?" I asked staring directly in his eyes. Patiently, I waited for any sign to point to recognition.

"I don't know a Marcus Tidwell. There's some type of mistake." His tears poured freely.

"Seven years ago you represented Marcus as a Juvenile. You willingly tricked hom into signing a pea deal in which he thought he'd go home. That wasn't the case. You conspired with Terrica Barr and through him to the wolves. Marcus ended up doing Seven years because of your treachery. Now its time to pay for your sin's." I leveled the pistol to his head.

"No, no, wait. I was blackmailed into doing that. Ms. Michelle Jackson caught me cheating on my wife and threatened to inform my wife if I didn't cooperate with her. I didn't have a choice in the matter. I did what I had to for the sake of my career and the sake of my family. I never wanted to throw anyone. Please you have to believe me." He cried.

"Even if I forgave you, your family would still be dead, and Marcus can never get back those seven years you took from him. See you later Tommy. That is, if I go to hell. BOOM!, BOOM! Two shots to Kennedy's heads exploding it on impact. The gore of the scene was enormously high. I kneeled down staring at Kennedy's only eye left and closed it with the hot barrel.

"Night, night Tommy." I walked out the house now thinking to myself that Marcus better not ever challenge my kill game or he'd end up never seeing light again. On top of that, even though Kennedy was marked off the list, another name had just been added. Ms. Jackson. I stepped outside making my way straight to where Marcus was parked. I got to the window and tossed the nine on his lap.

"Don't ever test my kill game, nigga."

"Is, is he dead." Marcus asked the inevitable.

"As a door knob. His wife and daughter too. However, there's more. I know who put him up to doing it." I smiled. That little bit of info peeked his interest.

"Who!"

"Someone by the name of, Michelle Jackson. I think she may have been the prosecutor.

"The she has to die along with everyone else. Why would she do this to me, I don't even know her."

"That's a prosecutor Marcus, that's not like killing a regular person tried to reason.

"I don't give a fuck what job she has. That bitch took my life for a reason."

"Alright, I can't tell you that I didn't warn you. It's your call in the end.

"Will you still help me?" Marcus looked at me with pleading eyes.

'I thought you'd never ask." I smiled deviously.

Chapter 9

-Chucky-

I sat in the house pacing the floor fully dressed in my Tuxedo awaiting Marcus arrival. It was now 7:45 pm. I'd calling Marcus phone since 6:30 pm only to continuously get the voice mail. Det. Pike was on my ass to hurry up and get some info. Now, when I finally called with a lead it was falling thought. All I could think of was losing my freedom. Suddenly, the phone rang. Reluctantly I answered it.

"Yeah!"

"We're at the Holiday Inn Charlie. Where's your boy?" Det. Pike got straight to the point.

"He's on his way just be easy." Even I didn't believe what I just said.

"I hope you're not shittin' me BOY! If so, your gonna be in central cell by morning. Are we clear?"

"Look here, cop! I told you he'd be there. Let your nuts go and be patient." I posed while also trying to speak with as much surety as I could. Then I got a glimpse of his other line clicking. Naturally, I thanked God.

"I have to take this call. You got one more hour for your boy to show up. You got me feeling as if I got the entire precinct in Montgomery County not to mention being out of our jurisdiction on a hunch. You know what I had to go through to cross State lines. You make me look like an ass and it's your ass. Click! He hung up. I looked at the phone thinking of my freedom and feeing it slowly becoming out my reach. If my freedom wasn't on the line I would have been killed this racist motherfucker. I had to get in contact with Marcus fast. I clicked the phone back on and attempted to call him.

"Hello." He answered on the second ring as if he was asleep.

"Man, where the fuck you at?" I've been calling you all day." I exploded.

"Wait, wait, wait watch your tone with me. First off, I don't have to check in with on one. Second; what the fuck do you want?"

"You forgot. Holiday Inn, at seven. Kennedy's party." I reminded him.

"Don't worry about it. We will get up with him another time. I got caught up with something."

"Then why the fuck you didn't call me?" I yelled knowing I would have to answer to Pike now.

"Look man, you're being real disrespectful right now. We'll talk when I get home.

"Fuck that, we gonna talk now." I demanded. My demands were met by the sound of a dial tone.

"Fuck!" I slammed the phone into the couch. Just as it hit, It began ringing again. I picked it up hopping it was Ashley or Marcus.

"Yeah!"

"Your boy not coming." Det. Pike stated.

"You said that I had an hour. Why the fuck you keep calling me?" I blasted.

"Did you hear what the fuck I just said? He isn't coming. Kennedy's body was found along with his family and your boy got away. An employee from Sir Williams Florist found them about an hour ago. Your boy spun you, Charles. He made his more, and sent you on a Goose Chase. You haven't given me a lint ball of evidence to bring him in. who's next on that list?"

"Terrica Barr, she's the Advocate." I gratefully replied.

"I'll be in touch. Oh yeah, don't try to leave town. I got men watching the airports and bus terminals. If I don't get this case your ass belong to me and everybody in D.C. Jail." Click! He hung up. Now my mind spun a hundred miles an hour wondering why Marcus would go without me. Did he not trust me? Did he just see a better option? We had definitely had to have a talk.

-Marcus-

Today had been extremely stressful. I was very grateful for Marcell. Had it not been for him, Kennedy would still be breathing. May the Devil burn his corrupted soul. Chucky on the other hand was really getting beside himself. What could possibly have him so angry; that I chose to go without him? Just because of his attitude, I had already made my mind up that even on the next one I would not include him. I was pulling up to the apartment when my cell phone erupted. I looked at the screen seeing an unfamiliar number, but decided to still answer it.

"Yeah!"

"That's a peculiar way to answer the phone." I recognized her voice immediately.

"Ahh, this have to be the lovely Ms. Amanda" I replied with a compliment.

"Your memory shows you favor, and the compliment is approached." I could hear her smile through the phone.

"I wasn't expecting your call, but glad I received it. How are you?"

"Fair, but lonely. My son just went with his father for the next two weeks. I was wondering if you would like to come over and show me exactly why you say that I'm your woman. For the life of me, I'm falling to come up with a good enough reason."

"I guess I gotta come check you out, sit you down and show you that I'm not just blowing smoke.

"Sounds interesting. I hope you can blow other things though." She seductively replied. I easily caught the hint and knew that she was trying to FUCK Hands down!

"Without question. You got a bad and dirty mouth, but I kind of like your attitude. Give me your address." At this point Chucky would have to wait. I had pussy on my mind and was determined to bask in it as soon and as much as I can.

"1429 Fairmont. Apartment 22."

"I'm on my way. I hope your mount still as dirty as it is now."

"Only one way to find out. See you soon, Mr. Marcus, I hope.

"Mr. Marcus! You funny as hell, I'll be there in ten minutes. I hung up with plans to blow a hole in her back. I bucked a U-turn and headed straight to her house. When I pulled up, I noticed a group of guys out front of her building. Once I parked, I made sure that my nine was at the ready and made my way into her building. Walking towards the building all eyes were on me. I took in that it was five of them and they all blocked the stairway.

"Excuse me." I stated. No one moved.

"Who you here to see, Moe?" A dark skin dude with a goatee and dreds asked.

"That ain't none of your business homes." His face bald. Just as he reached on his waist.

"DON!" Amanda yelled from her window. "Leave my friend alone!" She demanded.

"You know this nigga?" He pointed at me.

"Yes, let him up." Amanda replied.

"She just saved you slim." Don moved to the side.

"How do you know she didn't save you? They didn't stop making guns when you found one." I replied and walked pass.

"Under a different setting you wouldn't be walking now. Don't get caught in one, since your mouth writing checks. She not gonna be able to save you next time." Don warned. Seeing he could be more of a problem than I wanted to deal with. I said nothing and made my way inside. As I reached her floor Amanda stood in the doorway with some sky blue Booty shorts and a white belly shirt that said, I'm cumming God knew that I couldn't wait to experience the latter.

"Sorry about that. They're real protective over the territory around here." She smiled.

"I ain't tripping; I don't see none of that shit." Before she could reply, I pressed my lips against hers. Expecting my advance, she wrapped her arms around my neck just as out tongues began to entwine. Finally, we broke our embrace taking a deep breath.

"Let's get out of this hallway." She looked up into my eyes with a look of pure lust. She grabbed my hand leading me inside. I couldn't help but lust over her voluptuous ass as it swayed left to right. My dick couldn't help but bulge inside my pants. Amanda closed and locked the door.

"Put your hands on the door." I stated as a demand verses a mere statement.

"For what." She asked in defiance.

"Don't question me. Do what I said." I pulled my nine out and placed it on the table. Amada gave off a look of fear and reluctance she did as I told her. Slowly, I began rubbing her arms while pressing my hard-on on her ass. My hands moved to her waist as I moved across her body taking in her scent. Then allowing my hands to travel down her thighs. Soon, my hand stopped atop her mound. Heat poured from it. By my touch, I could hear a slight shutter escape her lips.

"What did I do to deserve this pat down?" Amanda spoke over her shoulder. I wrapped my arms around her waist and pulled her close.

"I gotta make sure you're not armed and dangerous." I then turned her around grabbing her by her butt cheeks lifting her into my arms. Easily, her legs wrapped around my waist. Our lips met again with our tongues igniting the sexual electricity between us. Amanda began clawing at my zipper anxiously trying to unleash the peak of her desire.

She reached her hand inside my boxers and began stroking me over so gently. I grabbed at her booty shorts, but was quickly put to a halt. She moved out of my grasp and walked off with a "come fuck me" glare in her eyes. I watched her ass giggle as she walked towards the back. I was so heated and standing there with my dick out that I would have followed her through the gates of hell for a shot of that pussy.

Like any man would have, I was on her heels. Reaching her bedroom Amanda stopped with her back to me and sensually rolled her shorts down her thick thighs. Her legs spread apart giving me full view of her neatly shaved pussy. Her slit glistered with secretion. She then crawled on the bed as if she were a lioness on the prowl. On all fours, with her back arched she looked back.

"Now come show me Why I'm your girl, and handle his pussy." She reached between her legs sliding two fingers in between her moistened lips. With a statement like that, she gave me all the push that I needed. I stepped out of my pants and moved towards the bed. While I was still standing, I palmed her ass spreading them apart before pushing the head of my rod through her vulva. As I entered, we both inhaled a deep breath of pleasure. With the wetness of her womb, I easily found a rhythm and beg and delivering calculated strokes.

"Oh yeah, baby right there." She moaned. My hands sunk into her ass cheeks.

"Who girl are you?" I said for lack of better words and experience. God this shift felt good! Even still all I could think of was Ashley.

"I, I, I'm your girl. Ohh God your dick is so big." She continued to moan louder and louder with each stroke, I delivered. Without asking, I turned her over on to her back holding her ankles in my palms. I aimed my manhood and plunged deep. I began long dicking her. It wasn't long before her head was lying on her ankles and she cumming.

"I'm cumming baby. I'm cumming. Do it harder. Ohh God Marcus. Do it har… I'm cumming Ohh…" I complied with her every wish and gave her every inch of my dick that I could. I could soon feel my load building to the point of eruption so I stopped and pulled out, laying on my back.

"Get your ass up here, and ride this motherfucker." I demanded. No more words were spoken. Amanda crawled on top without protest.

"No hold up." I put a hand to her stomach." Do it backwards." I Twirled my finger, and she smiled. Amanda turned around reached behind to position my tool to her tunnel. Once there she sat down. Seconds later she was bucking like a cowgirl. Every time she dropped, her ass would giggle turning me on even more. Her pussy made suction noises as she rode. My pressure began building immediately as I watched her gig ass go to work.

"I'm about to bust." I moaned. I gripped her waist pounding her pussy back everything she brought it up. Firmly, holding her ass in place I gained a steady rhythm. "I'm cumming again.," she resounded, with that I let off a well-needed load of semen within her walls. Both spent, we fell asleep in each other's arms through the nights covers Amanda went out well before I did. I could sleep late, knowing that I hadn't accomplished but one of my goals. I wouldn't be satisfied until my enemies heart stood at ease. I looked down at Amanda asleep on my chest on my chest and slid from under her. She stirred slightly but was back into a deep stupor in a matter of seconds. I quietly got dressed and saw myself out. Now I'd deal with Chucky.

-Chucky-

I was beside myself by Marcus lack of incorporating me into his plans for what he decided to do about Kennedy's fate. Although he knew nothing of my plans with Det. Pike. It made me look like I was playing games with not only my freedom, but with that sweaty ass pig, Pike. I was lucky that Pike didn't run ass in. My one chance at freedom was almost snatched from me in that quick of an instance. I wouldn't allow that to happen again. My plan was to put my foot down and demand that he kept it one hundred with me from here on out.

I sat in my lazy-boy in the bellows of darkness in my apartment. Vigorously, I filled my lungs with the exotic Marijuana plant called Purple Haze. With the natural stress of losing my freedom, I was forced to Physically induce relaxation to be able to think clearly. I guess that's why my Glock 40 sat on of my lap cocked and loaded. As the exotic plant took hold of my body, my mind replayed my conversation with Det. Pike. I could hear his words clearly.

I got your freedom in one hand and bitch ass in the other. Now I don't think you want to lose both. After the dicken that I gave her earlier today she's probably on my porch with her tail wagging and her out tongue out.

I couldn't bring myself to believe that Ashley would do that to me. Especially not with that Fat Bastard looking motherfucker. The clock read 10:57 pm. Every minute felt like an eternity as I waited on confirmation to step through the threshold of my apartment. No sooner than I extinguished the ember on the tip of the marijuana and placed it in the ashtray. Ashley walked in. without bothering to turn the lights on, she closed and locked the door.

"So is it true?" My voice sliced thought the silence of the darkness the room sat in.

"Agh, oh shit, Chucky. You scared the shit out of me." She flicked on the light." Why the hell are you sitting in the dark." She then took notice of the Glock sitting on my lap.

"Answer my fucking question." I demanded in a no non-sense tone.

"Is what true?" She placed a hand on her hip.

"Are fucking Pike?" I came out and said it. I couldn't see doing it any other way.

"I'm too tired for this shit, Chucky. I'm going to take a shower." Just as she attempted to walk off, I cocked the gun extracting a bullet from the chamber and it falling on to my lap. Hearing the rack, the all too familiar sound stopped her in mid-action. I then held the gun up for her view.

"Don't make me send one of these through you. Now answer my fucking question." I calmly yet firmly spoke.

"Why would you ask me something like that? You haven't never questioned me before. Why now?" She asked. I slowly rose from my chair and made my way towards her. Still, I clutched the Glock firmly in my palm.

"I'm gonna ask you one more time Ashley. Are you fucking him or not?" I asked through clenched. teeth.

"Figure it out." She rolled her eyes and attempted to walk off. her words infuriated me to the point where I grabbed her ponytail and slammed her into the wall. Through my nefarious anger, I placed Glock under her chin.

"Naw, bitch you figure it out. Now tell me what the fuck is going on.

"Chucky you done lost your goddamn mind. Get that gun out my face."

"I'm not doing shit until you tell me what I want to know." I pressed the barrel deeper in her chin.

"Fine, you want to know. Yeah, I fucked him. I fucked him because… SLAP! My anger soared before I could contemplate my actions causing me to backhand Ashley. She fell to the floor serving me a look of imprudence. Slowly, tears Streamed down her face.

"I've been faithful to you Ash. This is how you repay me?" I yelled just as Marcus stepped into the apartment. His eyes falling to the gun in my hand, then to Ashley on the floor holding her face.

"What's up Chucky, What are you doing man?" He asked in a dubious tone.

"Mind your business, Marcus. This is between me and her." I spoke over my shoulder not once taking my eyes off the love of my life.

"Man, you're tripping." Marcus snatched the gun from my hand, and took a step back." She is my business." By his last statement, my head snapped towards Ashley.

"You're fucking him too?" I asked in disbelief. Ashley then stood to her feet.

"Motherfucker I didn't it for you. It was a part of the agreement. I degraded myself for you. If you take time to listen before slapping me you'd see that I love your ass that fucking much to give myself to that sweaty motherfucker. I cannot believe you Chucky. The worst part is that I have to do it 20 more times, or not only is it your ass it's mines too." Listening to Ashley's words tore me up inside. I allowed my anger to piss in my ear making me deaf to any explanation.

"Damn, baby I'm so sorry." I reached out towards her, and she jumped simultaneously and took a step back.

"DON'T… TOUCH ME!" She yelled as I snatch her into embrace.

"I said I'm sorry Ash."

"Nigga she said don't touch her." Marcus pushed me towards the corner. "That's a female nigga. You ain't no better than the dudes my mother used to bring home when I was little. You ain't no better than Pearl. With each day that passes I'm really starring to see you ain't nothing but a bitch ass nigga." Being called a 'Bitch ass Nigga' infuriated me. I attempted to rush him, but was easily stopped in my tracks by the barrel of the Glock winking at me.

"Nigga act like you want to die." Marcus gripped the gun tighter.

"Damn, slim you gonna pull a gun on me?" I felt betrayed.

"No different than you putting one to Ashley head. You out of pocket slim. Get your head together man. You lunching."

"Naw, nigga you pack your shit and get out my spot."
I demanded.

"That won't be a problem. I was actually planning to
do that when I got here. This arrangement was bound to get
one of killed." He stated then tossed my gun on the couch. He
then moved to the room he had been staying in to pack up the
few things that he'd accumulated since coming home. I
looked toward Ashley who refused to make eye contact.
Refusing to give me any sign of forgiveness Marcus soon re-
emerged with two duffle bags.

"Let's go Ash!" As if on cue, Ashley followed behind
Marcus out of the apartment.

"Damn, I don't get no pussy either?" I yelled. Ashley
looked back with a mollified state and made her way out of
the door. For a second I wondered would she call of all bets,
but then remembered that she had something to lose too. She
was in deep as I was. Pike had us on the hook.

-Marcus-

It really moved something inside of me when I saw
Chucky placed hands on Ashley. I was now questioning what
that something was. Did I care about Ashley in a more than
platonic manner? Did I secretly wish that I had her heart the
way Chucky did? Or was it my childhood, watching men beat
on my mother. Watching various assaults and being
defenseless to prevent it. Regardless of what it was, I did

know that it was wrong. I couldn't stand back and watch Chucky take advantage of her felinity.

Another thing that peek my curiosity was what deal or agreement would make Ashley lower her morals and principles on the strength of her love for Chucky. I figured that whatever it was it had to be life altering. After tossing the bags in the truck of the BMW, I walked Ashley to her car.

"I really appreciate your help Marcus." She grabbed my hand.

"No Never. This whole thing is partially my fault. I should have told him." She began to cry. I placed my arms around her.

"Ashley, listen to me. It isn't ever your fault that a man puts his hands on you. You are a beautiful woman. All women are precious to the world. You are no different. Chucky was wrong in all aspects." I lift her chin up, and wiped away her tears with my thumb.

"I still should have told him."

"Told him what Ash? What could possibly be so important that he placed his hands on you. There is nothing that important." Now her vague statements were vexing me.

"There is so much more to everything Marcus. I can't get into it. Look I gotta go, thanks again." She leaned up and kissed me on the cheek then wiped her lipstick from it. She then stepped off towards her Acura. As she closed the door, I heard a window close behind me with a loud THUD! I looked up and saw Chucky standing there shooting daggers at me. He used his hand like a pistol and shot at me. It was at that point that I came to the realization that I may have to kill him, or get Marcell to kill him.

-Ashley-

I had been with Chucky for five years and never had he laid a hand on me. I sat in my car with Alligator tears streaming down my face. Here I was putting my career on the line and spreading my legs for this sweaty as Cracker. All for the man who would raise his hand and strike down at me. He made me question, was it all this worth loving him. Were all my sacrifices done in vein? All types of questions flooded my mind as I pulled up to my building. Walking in my apartment I was instantly disgusted at the sight of Pike seated only couch smoking a cigar and watching television.

"Heeyy, there go my chocolate sex toy!" He stood with a smile and outstretched arms.

"You know you're really wearing this popping up shit out, Pike. You got what you wanted, what's up now?" I wanted him to get to the point of his presence in my house.

"First off officer, Ashley. I got 20 more times to get what I want. Secondly, my dick is what's up and I think it's time for you to put it down." Det. Pike stated the walked toward me as he unbuttoned his slacks. I couldn't but noticed his penis growing to length by the second as he stroke it.

"By the look on your face Officer Ashley, I'd swear you liked old Detective Pike's tool." He stated in the third person with blatant arrogance and placed his hand on the back of my head. I said nothing and fell to my knees in front of who I claimed to be the devil himself. At first, he rubbed the head of his massive penis along my cheek and jaw line. Them found his way across my lips. I began to flick my tongue to fill it to capacity. Slowly, I would extract his muscle and flicked my tongue along the big vein on the bottom. I was using so much saliva that it began to drip down my chin. Before long, I was deep throating him like a champ.

"Ahh, ssss that's right Officer Ashley suck that dick. That's it, just like that." Det. Pike's face panted to the ceiling with his eyes close. I thought about clamping my teeth down as hard as I could, but knew the after effects would be greater than I was willing to pursue. Like a nice girl, I continued my task. Det. Pike grabbed the back of my head and commenced to fucking my mouth with minimal regard for my tonsils. I began to gag as his penis swelled up. His pace quickened, testacies smacking my chin. Abruptly, he pulled out splashing his load across my face. I was pissed, but defenseless to protest. I took it in stride, and allowed this man to disrespect me. To treat me like nothing more than a strung out prostitute. Det. Pike than stepped out of his pants the rest of the way.

"Go clean your face and meet me in the back." He tossed m a Kleenex and gave me his posterior. The Kleenex hit my face and stuck to one of the cascading globes of cum. I felt lower than low. Nothing more than a bottom feeder.

"Be quick about it, I'm not done with you yet." He then yelled over his shoulder, I did not reply. I simply did as told and wiped the semen off my face of shame.

Once I walked in the room, Det. Pike sat in a fold out chair facing the foot of my bed with maybe a foot in-between. He stroke his member allowing me to watch it grow at a firsthand account. As I started to walk towards him, he raised a hand in the air.

"Stop!" He pointed to the ground with his index finger. "strip!....Slowly. I want to watch." I gave no reply and complied with his wishes. As I began to undress, he continued to work himself. I could hear his breathing accelerate my the time I made it to my bra and thong.

"Now walk your sexy ass over here." I made my way over and stepped between him and the bed with my back towards him. He cupped both of my ass cheeks squeezing and spreading them.

"Have a seat on the throne, Officer Ashley." His grungy voice demanded. As I sat, he moved my thong to the side with his dick giving me its full attention in the form of the Washington Monument. As much as I hated to admit it, my pussy was soaked and wet, screaming for a beating. Descending on his lap, his dick spreaded my pussy lips. Easily sliding inside me with little restriction.

"Ohh." A moan escaped my lips against my protest. I didn't want Pike to know how much I was enjoying the way he handled my pussy. He gripped on tight to my waist guiding and bouncing my ass on his dick.

"That's right Officer Ashley, bounced that ass."

"Ohh God, Ohh God." I held on to the bed for leverage working his muscle. I could feel his dick in my stomach every time it disappeared inside my pussy.

"Tell me you like Det. Pike's dick. Tell me you like how Det. Pike stroke that bald kitty kat." Det. Pike began long stroking me. He would lift me up to the point of his dick reaching the tip of my entrance of my pussy then slamming my ass back down in rapid successions. At first, I refused to answer him, but when he started long dicking me I couldn't contain myself.

"Yes, Yes, I love. I love how you stroke me. I'm about to cum, Det. Pike make me cum.: I begged.

"Say please, Officer Ashley." Det. Pike voiced triumphantly as he toyed with me knowing he had broken me.

"Please! Please make me cum. I'm cumming." I begged and pleaded until I finally erupted on his shaft. I began watching his dick disappear in my pussy. I could see my cream coat his tool with glistening secretion. Again, his pace quickened with his penis head swelling up. He pounded my pussy harder and harder then abruptly stopped and tossed me to the floor. I expected to see his dick dripping with cum, but there was none. I could fell his juices seeping out of my pussy. He stood and made his way to the bathroom. When he appeared he had a towel wiping his dick off. when he was done, he tossed it to me. I continued to sit on the floor fucked and spent.

"Your boy had me on a wild goose chase tonight. He had me at the Holiday Inn with half the precinct on standby. Not to mention, in a jurisdiction outside of our own. Long story short, the murder never happened. At least not at the Holiday Inn. while we were there his boy or the suspect I should say, was at the victim's house. he murdered not only his target but his wife and daughter as well. the only reason I didn't lock his ass up is because there's supposed to be a list of people the guy plans to kill. I didn't get it this time, but I better get it on the next one." He warned.

"Who was the victim?" I could not help but ask. I placed on an oversized T-shirt.

"Thomas Kennedy. He made me look like a fool today, but that will not happen again. You're going to make sure it doesn't. because if it does, all bets are off. I don't have time for cat and mouse games. I want my murder, and I want it fast."

"Who is the suspect?" I had to ask, my life and career depended on it.

"Marcus Tidwell."

"What!" I couldn't believe Chucky would do this. It showed me that he was only loyal to himself.

"You say that like you know him." He stated. I was stuck for a moment.

"Well do you?" Det. Pike pressed.

"No! No I don't." I had no choice but to lie.

"Well get to know him." Det. Pike holstered his nine. "Until next time Officer Ashley. Keep it tight." He smiled and made his way to the front door. As he opened it Marcus stood before him.

"Oh my bad Ash. I didn't know you had company." Marcus stated.

"It's not a problem, he was just leaving." I assured.

"How you do, young man. Henry Pike." He extended his hand to Marcus.

"Marcus Tidwell!" By Marcus mentioning his own name my heart sank to the pit of my stomach. Det. Pike looked at me with blatant acrimony in his eyes.

"Get me my shit, Officer." He never gave me chance to respond as he gave me his back and stepped pass Marcus.

"I'll be seeing you Mr. Tidwell. You two have a productive night," Det. Pike tilted his hat and was off into the night. I then looked to Marcus.

"What's wrong Marcus is everything alright?" I asked, Marcus eyes remained on Det. Pike's departure.

"Who the fuck was that?" He asked completely ignoring my question.

"Come inside, its cold out." I pulled him inside. He walked in and made his way to my couch. His eyes now locked on me. That's when I realized that I had on nothing but an oversize T-shirt that only came to about mid-thigh. "Get your mind out of the gutter, Marcus." I slightly scolded.

"My bad Ash. I couldn't help myself. What's up with dude?" He continued not forgetting the vibe that Det. Pike gave him. Casually, he turned on the T.V.

"He's my college, and wants me to hurry and give him my report on some work stuff." I answered his question as vague and laconic as I could.

"Well I don't get a good vibe from him. Seems like he's on something. Anyway, look I need a place to crash tonight. I'll be out of your hair by morning."

"You're more than welcome here anytime." I smiled not minding his company at all. Mostly, because at least for tonight I would know that we weren't out there killing anyone. I will say that I was also confused. I didn't know whether to let him what I knew or let he cards Chucky dealt to fall where they may. I later figured that I would speak with Chucky about these new found aspiration.

"So that means, you sleeping on the couch." He joked.

"No! but you are. Let me get you a pillow and a blanket." Just as I got up, I turned the T.V. up to the news.

"We're in front of Criminal Defense Lawyer Thomas Kennedy's home, where it has became the scene of a triple Homicide. At this time, Police will say that the bodies were found by a Sir Williams Florist employee. Police are not releasing any further details. I'm Robyn Jackson, Fox Five." I looked to Marcus who appeared to be in deep thought.

"That's so terrible. How could someone do something so tragic?" I voiced waiting to acquire his reaction.

"Yeah that's pretty bad. What's up with that pillow?" He looked to me, changing the subject and took off his shoes. He acted as if he wasn't concerned at all about what happened. I choose to let it slide for now, and got him a pillow. I did make the summation that if Marcus did commit those murders and easily acted so non-chalantly only hours afterward, that his heart was colder than antifreeze on a winter's night.

When I returned with the blanket and pillow, he was stretched out on the couch, fast asleep. I noticed that his gun fell to the floor next to him. Carefully, I picked it up. I sniffed the barrel and smelled nothing but gunpowder. Meaning, it had been fired. I did not know what to think, so I placed it back and retreated to the back to take a shower and call it a night.

-Marcell-

It was 7:30 am and I was in the Court District in Northwest. Since Kennedy told me about Michelle Jackson. Both Marcus and I felt that she was the sole person that needed to be held accountable for Marcus doing that time. Plus, Marcus asked for my help. I knew if I left up to him his dumbass wouldn't know were to start. That's why I'm downtown at this very moment. I sat in front 555 Indiana Ave. otherwise known as Rat Central. This was the office of the AUSA's (Assistant United States Attorney's). I figured I could get a tail on Mrs. Jackson from here. I called inside to see if she was there. No sense in waiting out here, not knowing if she was in there or not. It rung about three times.

"District Attorney Office." W woman answered. I could hear laughter in the background.

"Hello, my name is Richard Edwards Attorney at law. I'm calling to speak with Michelle Jackson."

"I'm sorry sir, but Michelle Jackson got promoted to judgemenship two years ago."

"Is that so?" My mind began turning the possibilities.

I'm afraid so." You should try calling 500 Indiana Ave at the courthouse. That is where her chambers is located."

"Do you have that number?" I gradually asked.

"Yes, please hold. I was pissed the fuck off. I instantly knew that if she was a judge, it would be extremely difficult to get next to her. Sooner than later the woman returned on the line and after writing the number down I called immediately.

"You've reached the chambers of Judge Michelle Jackson. Currently I'm in trial, but if you would leave a detailed message I will be sure to get back with you at my earliest convinced." By the recording, I knew just where to find her. The courthouse, In trial.

Black: King Pawn D-4

All night I tossed and turned thinking of the imbroglio I put myself in. not only was I being had against my will, I was getting ready to be the orchestrator behind Marcus losing his life to jail for the reminder of it. I hadn't seen Marcus in seven years, but he was still my friend, and we shared that kiss that made me feel that there was something behind it.

Chucky had always been there for me while Marcus was away. I guess that explained why I fell in love with him. Now with Marcus being home, and the way Det. Pike was dicking me down. I was questioning that love and my loyalty behind it. I was truly caught between a rock and a hard place. My heart was being split in two between Chucky and Marcus. Then I thought that Maybe I could persuade Chucky to find a new target. If so, we could end this and break the stronghold that Det. Pike had on us.

I opened my eye and stretch out like a cat. Marcus was the first thing on my mind. I got out of bed and ran to the front room only to see that Marcus was gone. Sadly, my next thought was that he was going to kill again. The phone rung as if it knew what I was thinking, scaring me out of my thong. I rushed to answer it.

"Hello."

"How's our boy doing?" I was instantly disguised by Det. Pike voice.

"He's not here. I just woke up. He's gone." I replied through Det. Pike annoyance.

"You wouldn't be lying to protect this young man, now would you Officer Ashley?"

"he's not here Pike! You said there is a list of people who he's planning to kill, right?"

"What about it?"

"Well who's next on iy?" I got straight to the point.

"The next one is a woman named Terrica Barr; she used to be a Case Worker for CWS (Child Welfare Services).

"Well put 24 hour surveillance on her house. we need to keep her safe at all cost."

"Tell me something that I don't know Officer. I don't really like you involved in this case. Especially, after you lied about knowing Tidwell. Then he pops up on your doorstep. I shouldn't have to explain the depth I'll go to destroy you if you jack this case, do i?"

"No sir, I understand." I replied through clench teeth.

"Good! Happy Hunting!" Click! God I didn't know what to do. I flopped on the couch burying my face in my hands releasing my tears of confusion. Soon, I pull myself up to get dressed. I needed to see Chucky. He was the one who could stop all of this. The only one who could free me of my mistake. When I got there, I barged in to find Chucky in the kitchen.

"I can't believe you, Chucky."

"Look Ash, I said that I'm sorry for hitting you. I was wrong." He replied not knowing my angel.

"Motherfucker I'm not talking about me. How could you do this to Marcus?" I yelled in an unbelieving tone.

"I'm not about to talk about this." He walked off.

"You ain't gotta talk about it, but it's over with starting now." I pointed to the floor for emphasis. He stopped in his tracks and turned around filled with anger.

"Fuck you mean it's over? It ain't over till I'm out of that Crackers grasp." Chucky replied with his face inches from mines. Easily, he towered over me looking down into my eyes.

"This isn't right, Chucky." I pleaded with him.

"Bitch! This was your idea." He continued to yell.

"No! It was my idea for you to turn informer to clear your record. Not set up one of your child hood friends on a Marcus beef." I checked him.

"Well you planted the seed to make it grow. I'm not going to jail PERIOD!" Chucky attempted to finalize the conversation.

"You're one selfish son of a bitch Chucky. If you don't stop this and find a new agent or I'm tell him everything." I warned completely disregarding the repercussions.

"You do that and I'm taking you down with me. Your career will be up shits creek."

"Don't fuck with me, Chucky. I'm still the PO-Motherfucking –lice. I won't let you ruin Marcus life any more than it already has been."

"I ain't the smartest nigga in the world, but it sound like you fucking this nigga." Chucky shot, and walked into the bathroom.

"Chucky don't disrespect me. I have never cheated on you in our entire five years together. I am asking you Charles, No! I am begging you. If you love me, then pick another Target. He was my friend to." I pleaded to a closed door. I looked to the ceiling silently praying for help. Chucky turned and faced me.

"I do love you, but I love my freedom more. He doesn't mean shit to me when it comes to that. I'll kill for that." Chucky then looked me dead in my eyes. "Dig where

I'm at?" He spoke with much malaise and walked out the bathroom.

"Are you threatening me?" I was surprised by his words.

"No, just enlightening you on all of my options. This conversation is over and final. You can see yourself out." I could plead no more. What is done is done, and the wheels were turning and picking up speed. I could do nothing but bank my head low as I exited his apartment. Back in my car, I placed my head on the stirring wheel and cried.

"God what did I get myself into?"

Chapter 10

-Marcell-

White: King Bishop-F5

Once obtaining the information that I needed from Michelle's voice box. I made my way to the courthouse. How I saw it, was if she was in trial then there was only one place she could be.

I never liked leaving my gun anywhere but on my hip. Going in the courthouse, I knew that was the last place that I could bring it. Staying focus on the task at hand, I left it under the seat.

There was a small line outside when I arrived. Cautiously, I watched over my shoulder as I stood. I was standing in the belly of the beast and knew it. When my time came to I walked through the metal detector and raised my arms.

Next!" The old Marshal waved me through and called for the next in line. There were people everywhere. Young, old, some wore street clothes, and some wore pants suits. Nonetheless, it was crowded. The perfect camouflage to move. I made my way to the directory Board searching for Michelle Jackson's courtroom. Easily, I found it.

"Room 302." I said aloud. With courtroom being on the third floor, it pushed me deeper into the belly of the beast. This would force my moves to be more calculated for a difficult obstacle.

I stood on the escalator as it ascended me to the next level. Everywhere I looked; I saw U.S. Marshals dressed in there tan and blue uniforms of blue Jackets with bold yellow lettering. I felt like I was in a maze desperately trying not to bump into one of them. I easily surmised that this was not the place for a murder. It would be virtually impossible to commit the act and get away with it.

Once I made it to the third floor, the hallways went either left or right. Ahead of me, were the bathrooms. Just then, I saw a beautiful brown skin female. She reminded me of the actress Regan Gomez. She wore corn rolls that reached the middle of her back. Her complexion was golden and her dress was casual. Seeing her, I made my way to casually walk behind her. Her scent was intoxicating. Smells of exotic fruit filled her wake.   She then made another right into a courtroom. Reaching it, I looked on the door reading numbers 302 and the Honorable Michelle Jackson.

As I stepped in, the girl gave a short wave to the woman of the hour. Straight ahead sat The Honorable Michelle Jackson in all her beauty and prestige adorning the top of her throne with grace. I continued inside taking a seat directly behind the young girl who now sat with another female. Quietly, I zeroed in on Michelle atop of her perch.

I looked over to the defendant who visibly looked extremely nervous. I felt for him. Being in a courtroom behind the defense table was a stressful time. Personally, I felt that the entire judicial process was a scary situation. My prayer went out to the guy.

As the trial went along Michelle only sporadically intervene allowing the contestant ample freedom to present their case. My eyes never deterred from her. I could only see her. Mentally, I played a game with myself thinking what Michelle would do if she knew how close death was to her. How close and ironic her judgment Day was to date. Even being so close, I was so far away. The entire time I sat, the young girls in front of me laughed and conversed. I caught Michelle when she glance at the Regan Gomez look alike and she would quiet down, only for a moment before she continued. Soon, Michelle looked to be fed up.

"Okay ladies and gentlemen let's take a recess. We will continue in forty-five minutes. Please return on time. Do not discuss the case or read the newspaper." Michelle spoke in an authoritative tone. The Jury simultaneously stood methodically exiting the courtroom.

"You may take the defendant back." She instructed the Marshal. On cue, they did as told. Once they were gone, Michelle began her tirade.

"Melissa, get your ass up here now!" this was about to get interesting. I thought. Melissa stood and dropped a piece of paper. One in front of Michelle, she leaned forward like the Wizard of OZ.

"Tell me young lady. Do you know the significant value of being quiet while a trial progress?"

"I'm sorry mom. It won't happen again." She replied.

"You damn right it won't happen again. Get your ass out my courtroom, and you're not allowed back until you find some respect for it." Michelle ordered. The girl said nothing and stomped out of the courtroom. I was right behind her. Outside in the hall, I caught up with her.

"Excuse me, Excuse me miss." I yelled slightly jogging to catch up to her. By my voice, she turned around. "You dropped this." I handed her the paper.

"Thank you!" she replied.

"That's your mom in there?" I casually looked back.

"Yeah, she's pretty pissed." She slightly laughed.

"That's an understatement. Anyway, I'm Marcell." I extended my hand.

"I'm Melissa. Thank you for returning my paper." She began to walk off.

"Where are you going my good deed can't go unrewarded." I looked at her seriously.

" I said thank you; isn't that enough? Damn she was sexy, I thought.

"Hell no! But I would like to take you out and get to know you." I mashed the gas.

"Why do you want to get to know me? What makes me so special?"

"All I can say is that you're beautiful, and I thrive on not letting opportunity pass me by. I wish I could say more, but that is the reason I want to take you out, so I can learn everything about you. Only then I will be able to tell you why.

"You're smooth. I like that. Here is my number. Give me a call." She smiled as she handled it to me. All I could think of was jackpot!

➤ Schizophrenia

Chapter 11

-Marcus-

Black: Queen Knight-F3

My gut instinct was telling me Ashley was keeping something from me. I wasn't going to dwell on it though. At this point, I would wait till her skeleton stepped into the light, as all things must do. I had bigger things to deal with when I woke up this morning. I thought of Chucky and the altercation last night. I actually felt bad about it. After thinking about it, I surmised that I may have been wrong. They were a couple and I should have let them deal with whatever problem they may have amongst themselves. My sole purpose for staying with Chucky was to be close to my mother, and to handle my aspiration of revenge. I planned on apologizing to him. This was the purpose of my arrival to his apartment. As I walked up to the building's front steps, I heard a horn behind me.

"A Marcus!" I looked back to Marcell pulling up. "Come on, get in we gotta talk like yesterday." He pressed. I could hear the urgency in his voice so I hurriedly made my way down.

"What's up slim, why the rush?" I asked closing the passenger of the BMW.

"We're going to IHOP so we can talk there." He said nothing more as he hit the gas. The whole ride he remained quiet. My mind turned with different topics to help my curiosity. I could tell that he was in deep thought so I allowed him to remain that way until he was ready to converse. He ended up driving to Langley Park, MD and IHOP on New Hampshire Ave.

This section of Maryland, most would call Spanish Harlem because of the abundance of Latin Americans in the area. A low-income area for minorities. We pulled into a parking easily finding a place to park. My nine still tucked on my waist. As we stepped inside we were greeted by a young female with a big smile. Her hair pulled tight into a ponytail. By her over weight body, she looked as if obesity ran in her family. Nonetheless, she was cute.

"Welcome to IHOP. Table for one?" she asked.

"Uh, no! Table for two." I replied.

"Alright please follow me." The young girl grabbed two menus and led the way. Once we were seated, se set the menus on the table.

"Just give us two breakfast samplers please and two large orange juices."

"Will that be all?" She continued.

"Did we ask for anything else?" Marcell snapped giving her a cold glare that spoke a thousand words in silence. His candidness threw her demeanor off.

"Your orders will be ready shortly." She rolled her eyes and snatched the menu's. Each step in her departure said acrimony.

"Why you do her like that." I slightly laughed.

"Fuck that little bitch. I got bigger shit on my plate and so do you." He revealed.

"Speak your mind my friend. The suspense is killing me." I joked.

"I took the liberty of getting the jump on Michelle." He paused for my reaction.

"Well!" I calmly waited for the rest.

"Well. I got some good news and some bad news. The bad news is that Michelle is no longer a District Attorney; she's a Judge now. That alone raises the stakes. The moment we kill that bitch, the entire Metropolitan Police Faction , and political big heads are gonna go crazy and going to fight for someone to take the fall for it. Even if only for the city of Washington. They won't let her death turn into a cold case." Marcell reasoned.

"I don't see how any good can come of that. She might be impossible to get at." I surmised.

"No one is impossible to get at. The good news is this." He slid me a piece of paper.

"Okay it's a phone number. Who does it belong to?" I wasn't getting it.

"That number belongs to Melissa Jackson. Michelle's daughter." Marcell leaned back folding his arms across his chest with a broad smile basking in his own self-praising glory. I still wasn't impressed, so I slid the number back to him.

"Okay so what's your plan? How do you get at Michelle from this number?"

"Come on Marcus. WAKE THE FUCK UP." He placed his index to my forehead. "If I play my cards right, at the very least I could obtain Michelle's home address. If not, I can at least use her daughter to lure her out as bait." As he spoke of the possibilities, he smiled devilishly. With this number Melissa may have just killed her mother herself. Either way it goes she's a dead woman walking." Marcell spoke with surety. He seemed confident he could get it done. Hell, he was doing me a favor. By now, the waitress had returned with our plates. Once setting them down she looked at me.

"Anything else." Her neck rolled with each syllable. I thought to myself; this bitch has to be straight out of the projects. Her entire oral said Hood rat!

"Yeah, we're cool." I replied. She rolled her eyes yet again and stormed off.

"That bitch doesn't even realize how easy it would be to put a bullet in her head and make her late for work." Marcell spoke in a tone even octave more than a whisper.

"Calm down my friend. Focus on the task at hand." I smiled. Tell me more about Michelle. "I asked and began eating my plate.

"After Michelle, all that's left would be Terrica Barr right." Marcell asked.

"Yeah I think I want to do that one myself. Her murder is personal to me. She's a bigger factor in all of this than Kennedy and Michelle. She pretended to care about my well-being. Gained my trust only to nail me to that cross like Jesus Christ. I want to look in her eyes when her heart stop beating." I felt my anger boiling. Marcell began to laugh."

"You sounded really good Marcus. Almost as if you stood in a mirror and practiced that. Yet again, I will continue to stress to you my dear Marcus." He leaned forward. "You ain't no killer. As much as you may want to be, it just isn't in you. Then you want to talk to me,, of all people. ME! Like you certified at this shit. What the fuck would you have done had I not stepped in? Kennedy and his family would still be alive." Marcell killed my thought.

"So because I didn't kill Kennedy and his family I can't voice my aspirations?" I asked for clarity.

"Nooo, no, no I'm not saying that at all. I'm just saying for you to be you, and allow me to do ME! Then and only then, will your vengeful heart be place at ease." Marcell continued with his arrogance causing my blood to turn hot.

"Man. Fuck what you talking about. My gun go off just like yours. What you think they stop making guns and trigger fingers when they made yours?" my top was about to blow.

"That's exactly not what I'm saying. Your gun can go off like mine, but the question is will it? Although you very capable of doing what I do, so it's a ten year old. Meaning you may be physically able, but mentally you're softer than a fat bitch pussy. To be able to kill mercilessly with no regrets, it takes this." He pointed to his temple. "It takes the mentality of a cold hearted motherfucker to be a killer. A single individual with a heart black as tar and cold as ice to be what I was born. So yeah, you might have a trigger finger. You might even have a gun, but you don't have the mechanics to be what I am." Marcell started to eat his meal silently finalizing the subject.

I couldn't say a word from my rising temper. My teeth gritted with vigor. I hadn't been this angry since the day I shot pearl. Containing it became a task in itself. All I could do was stare at Marcell as he ate with a u shit-eating grin on his face. Then the waitress returned.

"Here's your check. Will there be anything else?" She asked with attitude. From the deepest bellows of my existence, I shot up from my seat grabbing her ponytail. Simultaneously whipping out my nine and placed it under her chin "BOOM!" The bullet exited the top of her head. As her body fell, I looked to Marcell.

"Stupid nigga. Look at all these people. Get the tape you dumb motherfucker." Marcell ran to the back of the restaurant and quickly returning with a CD and a VHS tape. Frantically, he grabbed a small trashcan and tossed out plates in it. In the process spilling orange juice on the table. Hopefully erasing any evidence of us being here.

"Let's go." He yelled and we ran out the IHOP.in the BMW, we hit Piney Branch RD straight to Northwest D.C I couldn't believe what I did, but was glad that I did it. Now maybe Marcell would show me some respect.

Chapter 12

-Chucky-

I was immensely disappointed to myself for letting my anger get the best of me last night. The key to my freedom with Marcus. I was praying that I hadn't burned my bridge with him. Even if I hadn't I wasn't sure if he trusted me enough to divulge any information to me about his plans. I had to find a way to get back in good graces. My life depended on it. Literally! With all that had been going on, I hadn't made a dime. Thinking so, I thought of Don and figured that he had to be done with his work. It never took him long. I decided to call him and see what was up.

"Hello!" He answered.

"What! Who the fuck is this?" Don sounded agitated.

"This is Chucky, nigga. I was calling to see if you were ready for me. I'm back.'

"I don't know what you talking about." Click! He hung up. I looked at the phone not knowing what to make of it. At times Don could be difficult to deal with. I figured a face meeting would be more receptive. I grabbed a brick and hopped in my car headed for Fairmont.

The streets were all I had and knew, so I had to get money. Whatever he didn't get I'd go see my other people and dump it off on them. Either way it goes, I was going to get money by any means necessary. I pulled up noticing Don out front standing with Bishop and Koofi and some random female. I made a U-turn and found a parking space. I never liked coming around here, so I was sure to always feel the tension in the air, but wasn't sure why. Once I was up on the crowd Don whipped out chrome. 50 cal. Desert Eagle.

"Bitch nigga. What the fuck you doing around here?" He was up on me with the quickness. His advance didn't give me a second to arm myself. I stood there terrified with my arms up. The triangle barrel rested on my jaw line.

"I, I came to see if you wanted some coke.

"You just called me. If I wanted something, I would have said it. Now why the fuck are you here?" He asked again, but I didn't know what to say.

"I'm telling the truth. That's why I came." WACK! Don sent the barrel crashing over my temple. Blood shot out the gash above my eye. "Aggghhh, come on 'S' I'm telling the truth. I pleaded.

"A Bishop, check this nigga for a pistol." Don ordered, Bishop complied easily relieving me of my weapon.

"Now strip nigga. You better not have no wire on." He stated with heavy gun winking at me.

"Come on S; don't do this to me slim. You know me." I continued to plead. My pleas fell on deaf ears. Don began to pistol-whip me until I was dazed.

"Now strip Nigga. Next time you won't have the chance." Slowly I began to peel off every article of clothing I had on in the middle of the block. Soon I was down to my boxers and socks yet still holding my car keys.

"See I told you. I don't have shit." I held my right elbow with my left hand completely embarrassed.

"Bitch Nigga, I said STRIP! BOOM! Don released a shot to the ground next to my feet. The shot scared the shit out of me. I then removed the rest of my clothing as quick as I could until I was ass naked.

"Now that I know you don't have wire on I feel a little more at ease. The only reason why I'm going to let you walk off this block is because if you're a rat they might be watching you.

"A rat! Nigga you know me." I defended, WACK! Don hit me again.

"Yeah, I know you, I know you a sucker ass nigga. Just so you know. I see you get bagged when you pulled off. Then this morning you call my phone talking reckless. How the fuck you out of jail anyway? Matter of fact get you bitch ass from around here before I say fuck them people." He took one step towards me. That was all the initiative I needed to get up and haul ass to my car. Never have I been so disrespected. I made a mental note to see Don again and I knew exactly how I was going to do it.

I drove straight home to tend to my wounds. The drive was trying in itself. The entire ride I fought to not pass out behind the wheel or even worse swerve in front of a police car. I swore to myself that Don would pay for this. I would see to it that he did.

I pulled up at the same time as Marcus mother. Seeing her brought my mind back to what I could do to get back in Marcus good graces. As if a light went off in my head, I got an idea. I ran to my stash and retrieved a thousand dollars and ran back to catch her before she made it in the house.

"Mrs. Karen, Ms. Karen." I yelled running after her as she made it to her door. She stopped and turned. On sight of my battered face, Mrs. Karen inhaled with a hand to her mouth in a state of shock.

"Oh my God, Chucky. What happened to you?"

"I got jumped and robbed earlier this morning." I said out of breath.

"Well come on in here and let me clean you up. Marcus isn't with you is he?" she looked up the street.

"No ma'am. I haven't seen him this morning."

"Well come on in." Mrs. Karen walked in her house with me taking up the rear. Her house hadn't changed a bit since I used to frequent the residence as a child. Even now, it still held gloomy aura about it. It also made me miss my childhood.

"Have a seat in the living room. I'll be right there." Mrs. Karen directed walking in the living room; I immediately noticed the massive amount of pill bottles on the table. I couldn't tell the type they were but there were a lot to say the least. I picked up one for closer inspection.

"It's not polite to snoop around people's house." Mrs. Karen stated. Startled, I placed the bottle back down.

"Sorry, Mrs. Karen."

"Get on over here so I can clean you up and get out of here." I sat in the chair as she looked me over with her first aid kit. "Look at your face boy you're gonna need stitches." She stated setting the first id kit down. She began to work as if it were second nature, I saw now as good as any time to accomplish what I came here for. Mrs. Karen put on her gloves as she began to tend to my wounds.

"Ms. Karen, can I ask you a question?" I asked as if it were bothering me.

"What is it child?"

"Ouch!" She struck the needle through my gash. "Why is it you hate Marcus so much?" Abruptly she stopped and looked at me.

"You want your face stitched up or you wanna get up in my business?" she put a hand on her hip.

"I'm sorry, Mrs. Karen. It's just that I'm around him and it's sad because even he doesn't know why. I want to help him get some type of clarity and understanding that is all. I'm not trying to get in your business. I just want to help my friend." Mrs. Karen let out a deep sigh and continued her work. "Ouch!" she stuck me again.

"You know it's a damn shame, as smart as my boy is he couldn't figure it out on his own."

"Is it really that simple to figure out why a mother despised her own son? Ouch!" I jumped at the pain.

"You think I just got up and spit that little nigga out and said I hate you? Do you really think that I'm that heartless? She stepped back and looked at me.

"No ma'am." I replied. Again she continued.

"But I will be honest with you since you actually had enough courage to ask me. That's some that Child Advocate couldn't ask me."

"You mean Terrica Barr?" I asked.

"Yeah, that bitch! She kept coming here trying to persuade me to take him back. Eventually, I sat her down and explained my story to her. Once I told her, that bitch never came back and I was grateful. Marcus was a chapter I was happy to close." She said in a tone of relief.

"Ouch!"

"It started when I was 15 years old. I grew up with my father and mother. The only reason they were together were to support each other habit. You see, both of them were addicted to heroin. I used to watch them shoot dope in various parts of their bodies like it was no tomorrow. Had it not been for my aunt, I would have been passed out. She took care of me.my Aunt Penny was my savior. She couldn't have kids so she treated me like I was her own.

"Ouch." I continued to listen.

One day while my aunt was over our house she was yelling at my mother who was sitting at the kitchen table counting a pile of money. There had to be at least a hundred thousand or better. I'll never forget that day. I remember it like yesterday; I was eavesdropping from my room door.

"Angie is you crazy. You think somebody saw you?" Penny was worried.

"No, all his workers were gone."

"His workers? Who did you steal this from?"

"I stole it from Rasheed's stash house a few hours ago, and be quiet before someone hears you. I saw him take the bag into the house, so I waited for him to leave and I broke in. after searching for a little bit, wa-la." Angie waved at the money like she did a magic trick.

"Oh God Angie, what if someone saw you? Penny voiced her concern.

"They didn't Penny. Stop worrying so much. Plus, who's gonna believe an old Dope fiend bitch like me pulled it off.

"Angie, you have to get out of the streets girl. They're going to kill you if you don't. if not for me then do it for Karen. Take that money and get a new life. A new beginning. This may be your second chance at life Ang." My aunt Penny loved my mother. She always tried to get her out of the streets, but the streets had her in a vice grip.

"You know what sis, you're right. This is my second chance and I'm gonna take it" I cried tears of happiness when I saw my mother pick up her needle and break it in two. Those same tears of happiness were short lived. By the breaking of the needle two masked men kicked in the door waving guns with silencers on them.

"There that bitch go right there." His voice sounded so familiar. I watched as he easily, without hesitation aimed his pistol at my mom's head and shot her twice. Blood and brain matter covered the money.

'Anngggie!" My Aunt Penny screamed walls of lost and fell to her knees at my mother's side. Insanely, she attempted to push the blood back in my mother's head, yet it was to no avail. Then as cool and placid as a summer night after a heavy storm, the same masked men stopped behind my Aunt Penny placing the barrel to her cranium.

"I never like you no way." Boom! Her body fell limp. Her eyes still staring directly at me, yet staring at nothing anymore.

"Okay slim, you got your money back and I killed my wife to prove to you I had nothing to do with it." I heard one of the gun men say.

"You should have been involved, maybe she'd still be alive." I watched the other masked man shoot the other two times. Seeing that, I whimpered and drew the attention of him. Then slowly, he aimed his pistol at me and removed is mask. "Rasheed!" I voiced. The look on his face was one of hunger.

"Take off your clothes."

"What!" Twip! He shot the bed.

"Bitch I said take off your clothes!" He yelled, and I jumped as I complied. Rasheed took my womanhood before I understood what my womanhood was.

When he was done, he wiped himself on his shirt. Once he situated himself, he rose up and shot me two times in the chest. He left me for dead, but didn't check to see if I was. He took his money and left. He was gone but left something behind. I was pregnant with Marcus. I made it to the phone and dialed 911 and everything went black. I woke up in the ER. Once I gained some form of my health to talk, I went to the police and was set to testify against him. I never got the chance to because he took a plea bargain and received 26 years. Being raped by Rasheed hurt me to the core. It got worse when I found out that I was pregnant by him. Thus came Marcus born into the splitting image of him I saw nothing but the man who killed my mother and my father along with my savior Penny.

The hatred I housed for that man remained alive and it live through Marcus. My very own son. For a long time, I felt no one loved me. That's when I met Pearl and Marcus killed him. That caused me to hate him more. All I could see was my father taking someone I loved away from me again. After Pearl, I met a guy name

"Smooth James Pride. All, the woman loved him, but he was mine. He was beautiful, inside and out." Karen smiled at the thought and stared off into space.

I soon learned that everything that glitters ain't gold. James was a sick man. Unbeknownst to me he was infected with the HIV virus. I was in love that the thought of using a condom never crossed my mind. That mistake, I am forced to live with for the remainder of my life. I became diagnosed with the virus three years ago. I live in pain from the sins of my mother. So you see now Chucky, I could never love Marcus. To love him, would be the killer of my family or maybe in a way forgive him. At the least, it would be loving his offspring. An act I have no choice but to despise with aversion."

She pushed the last hit of tape over my wounds. When she finished I had to catch myself from dropping a tear. "Damn, Mrs. Karen, I feel bad all that shit happened to you. So Marcus doesn't know a thing about any of this?" I asked already knowing the answer.

"No I could never look him the eyes without seeing Rasheed looking back at me." She wiped her cheeks. I stood and reached in my pocket for the one thousand dollars.

"Ms. Karen! My reason for coming here today…" I paused for a second and gathered my thoughts. "After hearing your story, I wanted to ask you to take this thousand dollars. In return, for you to at least talk with him. Tell him everything that you told me. Even if you can't look him in the eye, just at least shed some light on his presumption of your reasoning. Your invective and evasiveness is killing him slowly. I'm not asking you to love him. All I'm asking is for you to explain why the love he showed you never reciprocated. Just why?" she looked at the money with her mind clearly contemplating my wishes.

'I'm sorry chucky. If I take that money, it would be equivalent to putting a price on my family and, my virginity. Not to mention Pearls life, and now my own demise. You can't put a Band-Aid on a wounded heart. It eventually falls off." Karen reasoned and pushed the money towards me.

"I understand Ms. Karen. I guess it's time to leave." I took a step to the door. "Thank again."

"You're welcome Chucky." She replied after I closed the door. After hearing the story, I felt a sense of pity for her. I couldn't imagine what Marcus was going through under the same room without the love of a mother. Nor could I relate to the emotion that Ms. Karen felt every time she laid eyes on her only son. All I could do was refrain from causing any more pain than I've already endured. At that moment, I decided that I would have to get Det. Pike a new target. I couldn't be the hand that giveth that cup to Marcus. My heart wouldn't allow it. On the other hand, Don would get his hand called for. Karma was a bitch that came back around every time she left. Ultimately, he would reap what he sowed By Any Means Necessary.

-Det. Pike-

I sat at my desk in front of my computer looking up Marcus Tidwell on Goggle. I was only half expecting to find something useful. I felt that nothing beats a failure but a try, so I continued my quest. At least 15 Marcus Tidwell's popped up. I briefly scanned through all of them until I seen one of the names associated with the Washington Post. As optimistic as I could, I caressed the mouse ad clicked on it. Instantly, the screen changed to an article inside the Washington Post called Metro. The article was dated September 12, 2008. Seven years ago. I voiced to myself. I began to read the title of the article.

"33 year old male identified as Cortez "pearl" Humphrey was murdered last night by a 12 year old boy…" My reading was interrupted by my colleague barging into my office without knocking.

"Hey Pike! Henry greeted. Henry was a beat cop desperately trying to make to make it to Detective.

"Don't you know how to fucking knock?" I yelled looking up from the screen.

"Sorry sir, but Chief Lanier wants to see you in her office, pronto."

"Yeah well I'll be there when I get ready." I replied just as Chief Lanier bent the corner.

"Then I hope you ready now! My office right now Pike!" the chief spun on her heels not giving me a chance to reply.

"Bitch!" I mumbled and fell en route to her office. When I stepped outside, all eyes were on me.

"What the hell ya'll looking at?" I barked. Simultaneously, they all began acting as if they were busy tending to various task. "Nosey ass crabs." I continued my stride toward the top of the food-chain before going political. At least Chief Lanier was white woman talking to me the way she did. I would never stayed tight-lipped had she been a black woman. No matter what rank she held. When I reached her office there was a white man sitting with her adjacent to the chief desk. Blonde hair, blues eyes, crisp suit. Three piece at that. He looked like he was of a higher authority than our beloved chief.

"Sit." The chief used her pen to point to the chair next to prince charming. He authoritative voice let me know she meant business. This had to be about the Kennedy murder. I thought.

"Detective you used city funds and resources to go outside of our jurisdiction on a hunch. To stakeout an event that didn't produce anything but drinks and traffic violations. Then how I hear it you were receiving Intel from God knows whom. Telling you a murder was going to happen. Then while you were there, the Kennedy family was murdered in the District. I don't know where you're getting your information from Detective, but the next time you use unauthorized resources outside our jurisdiction you'll be on traffic day.

"I received information that Kennedy was to be at that Holiday Inn. That was my reasoning behind going outside out jurisdiction. Trying to save a life. If I'm wrong, I don't want to be right. I have a suspect already, and how I'm getting it from my Rat he's not done yet. Not to mention, I think I know his next target.'

"Sounds like you're trying to catch a murderer after act instead of preventing it from happening." Blondy spoke up with his legs crossed and index finger along his side of face.

"And who the hell are you?" I questioned looking at him with conviction.

"Det. Pike let me introduce you to Agent Maxwell Courtney. He's been sent by the FBI as a liaison upon hearing about the Kennedy massacre. He was deployed here to oversee the investigation.

"How you do detective?" Agent Courtney greeted with an arrogant smile and a two-finger salute.

"I put the work in for this Chief. He ain't taking my case." I stated with worry washing over me.

"Ease yourself detective. I'm not here to take your case. All I'm here for is overseeing. Now if you give me reason to take over, I will. Like if another body drops. Catch my drift."

Det. Courtney shot the subtle warning Det. Pike caught it, mid-stride.

"This is bullshit Chief." I was livid.

"It's out of my hands Detective. I'm sorry."

"I would like the name of your suspect, and any evidence along with whatever case file you've already created. I also want it by lunch tomorrow. As of now, I'm not involved in your little case. Personally, I believe the whole thing is beneath me. I am out of your way until you force me in it. Do you understand, Detective?"

"Loud and clear." I stated through clench teeth. God knew how bad I'd love to put a bullet between both of their eyes. I had to play ball though, if I wanted to keep this case.

"Good, no more stunts like you just pulled. If so, I'll re-assign the case in totality. I will not allow you to make me look bad, detective. You can leave now, and be sure to get Agent Courtney what he asks for."

"Will do Chief. You two have a nice day." Again, I gave a fictitious smile and departed the office with only thoughts of that disloyal nigger, Chucky.

-Marcus-

"Fuck! Fuck! Fuck!' Marcell banged on the dash boarded with his fist. "How stupid could you be Marcus? You see how many people were in there. NO! Fuck that. You see how many witness were in there?" he yelled. I couldn't say anything in defiance or to negate anything that he said. He was right. I acted foolishly and solely on impulse, but I wouldn't let him drag me through the mud about it.

"Alright I hear you I fucked up. What is done is done. Ain't no bringing her back. You got the tape anyway, we should be good." I tried to reason.

"Bitch nigga, should he ain't never good." Still he yelled invectively. As I stopped at the light, I'd had it. I snatched the nine off my waist simultaneously grabbing a handful of his shirt digging the nine in his cheek.

"I had about enough of your mouth, BITCH NIGGA! It's over with, the bitch is dead and I killed her. Now we play it by car. You're not going to keep dragging me about it. Dig where I'm at?" nothing but a bad situation behind his words.

"That's right Marky Mark. Get tough! Get Gangsta! That's what I'm talking about." I released my grip and continued across the D.C/Maryland state line. The remainder of the ride remained quiet. Seeing Chucky's building was like grazing the finish line.

"Look man I'm about to go get some shut eye before I call Melissa to set that date up." Marcell informed.

"Alright get at me later when you find out something." I replied. We pounded fist and he was out. He took the stairs up to his apartment while I made my way to Chucky's apartment. I hoped he wasn't still fucked up at me. I reached the apartment door and knocked. When he opened the door,

I was surprised to see his battered face. He looked like Martin Lawrence on his old sitcom Martin When he fought Tommy "Hitman" Herns.

"Damn, Chucky what the fuck happened to you." His face was brutal to the eyes.

"I got in a car accident." I knew he was lying, but opted to let it go. We both knew somebody whipped his ass. Chucky may have felt insecure about whatever he went through. If he said he was in a car accident then "I'd like to see what the car looked like." I said to lighten the mood.

"Look man, I'm sorry I snapped at you like I did the other night. I was out of line." Chucky apologized.

"Man, I'm not tripping on none of that. We boys. That hit small slim. We bigger than that." We slapped hand and gave each other a many hug. "Have you talked to Ashley?" I asked.

"Yeah, but she fucked up at me, I messed up big time with her Mark. We been together for five years and I have never laid a finger on her. She's devastated right now." Chucky took a seat on the lazy-boy. He used both hands running his fingers through his hair if it would remove the anxiety he was enduring.

"Chucky, Ashley loves you to death, slim." Everybody makes mistake and if she love you like she say she do. That love gonna over power the mistake you made. I voice some sound reasoning.

"I hope you right Marky man, I hope you're right. He sat back in his chair and took a deep sigh. "Look man I might need your help on something. There is a spot off 14th street called Fairmont. There are two main people out there. One of them name is DON, and the other is Head. They run the stripe. I need that strip Marcus. I need to elevate myself.

"Why don't you just kill them both and be done with it? The block will be yours." I naively spoke.

"It ain't that easy. Both Head and Don are head bussers and both street conscious. I can count countless crews that are certified, that had beef with them, yet they still breathing. That should tell you a lot." Chucky explained.

"Come on Chucky you putting me in a fucked predicament. You know I got my own thing that I'm working right now. The Advocate still living." I opted not to say anything about Michelle.

"I'm not saying right now at this very moment. Just when I call I need you there for me."

"What's your plan?" Chucky then smiled at my interest.

"Left hand was the right hand both hands wash the face. I'm going to set it up for don to kill Head and take the fall for it. Killing two birds with one stone. Block open, shop open. Once we take the block, I'll supply you the work and you can run the operation. We split everything 60-40 until you can pay for your half of the re-up. Then we go 50/50, It is money up there to get and I'm trying to get it. So what's up slim, you with it?" Chucky was becoming excited by his thoughts. I will admit his plan sounded logical. Not giving me a reason to say no!

"You been there for me since the day that I walked out that hell hole. Why wouldn't i?" We stood and slapped hands with the same one arm hug as if signing a contract in blood at the dotted line. Like he said, there was money to be made and like Chucky, I wanted to make it

Chapter 13

-Marcell-

After all this time, I thought Marcus was a straight up pussy. Finally the nigga was coming out of his shell. I was glad because that soft shit was really starting to rub me the wrong way. When he pulled the gun on me, I wanted to leap for joy. With that, I knew that soon Marcus was gonna be as cold hearted and cold -blooded as I was. Well maybe not all the way, but that nigga was getting there real fast.

After getting me some shuteye, I woke up about 9:30 pm. The first thought that came to mind was Melissa. Thinking of her made me view her as a mountain in 120 degree heat, with a pot of gold at the top in the middle of an oasis. A feat worthy of high reward. To win her trust meant certain death for not only Michelle but Melisa as well. I grabbed my pants in search of the small piece of paper she wrote her number on. Finding it, I punched it in on my cell phone I anticipated the encounter with grave urgency.

"Hello." Her voice like the sound of Gabriel's voice.

"How are you, Melissa?" I cordially greeted.

"I'm fine, but may I ask whose calling?" She slightly laughed.

"My apologies, its Marcell, we met at the courthouse. " I anticipated her recollection.

"Okay, how are you Marcel? I was actually just thinking about you."

"Oh really, well I hope the mere thought of me was soothing to the mind."

"You sound so conceited, but don't flatter yourself. I was just thinking how I met you in the courthouse. You were dressed like a street dude, yet even after finding out my mum is a Superior Court Judge, you still persuade me. Most street dudes run from me for fear of some type of prosecution." She laughed.

"Then that should tell you something."

"And what is that?"

"I'm not s street dude. I also could care less about some type of prosecution for attempting to court a woman of your caliber, but if it is a crime to do so, then she may as well mark me as a career offender. Besides, my criminal days are behind me." I laughed at my own humor. My laugh was contagious, as I heard Melissa replicate the aspect of the emotion of happiness she was feeling.

"You're funny Marcell. I like a man, who can make me laugh. What did you mean by your criminal day were behind you?" she asked. I thought about lying but figured that she might have her mother do a background check on me and blow my cover.

"I did a little stint as a juvenile for robbery." I revealed and slightly prayed she didn't run.

"Well I pray that you learned your lesson." She chastened.

"I did. For the record, I appreciate you for not judging me about my past."

"I appreciate you for being honest." She laughed again.

"I love a woman who is not too stuck up to laugh. You have a pretty smile and I enjoy seeing it."

"Oh no I'm far from stuck up to laugh. I am very down to earth. I feel if you're not smiling then you're sad about something. I like to look for the greater things in life." She expressed in.

So tell me Ms. Judge Daughter. What are the chances of me seeing you tonight?" My stomach churned with the excitement of the cat and mouse game we were engrossed in.

"Well, it's kind of late. I don't see how a couple of hours of conversation could hurt my morning schedule. Only if you promise to have me home by 12:30 am"

"I promise, cross my heart and hope to die. Where can I pick you up at?" The moment of reckoning. If she gave me her home address then she and Michelle would be dead by morning.

"Meet me at 10:15 in front of the Gucci shop on Wisconsin Ave"

"I know that. We're not going there. Meeting me there is nothing more than a precautionary measure. I don't know if I trust you yet. Nor do I know your intentions. I am still a judge's daughter who oversees criminal cases and used to be an ex-prosecutor. Many people would see harm brought to my mother or me to get to her. Because of these reasons I'm very selective with whom I entrust with the address where my heart lay." She replied.

"Your wished are respected. I'll see you at 10:15 pm."

"Thank you. I'll see you then." Click1! I could see now that this will be a tad bit more trying than Kennedy was. Michelle taught her daughter well. Mellissa could have easily pulled the trigger to her and her mother's demise. In a way, I was a little happy she didn't. It made the chase of it all more alluring.

"It didn't take long for me to get dressed. I choose some dark blues Guess jeans and a black and Grey Hugo Boss sweater. I threw on my leather jacket and a black and grey Redskin hat to see it all come together. Not too much, not too little, but smooth as a motherfucker. Like your first sip of Remy XO when it rolls down your throat.

I hoped in my ride and was on the road by 9:50 pm. I couldn't wait to see her. Melissa was a bad bitch all the way around the board. I made a mental note to fuck her fine ass before I killed her. I made it to the Gucci shop at 10:15 on the nose. Instead of sitting in a car ten o' clock at night in Georgetown I opted to get out and wait. I tucked in my nine on my hip and made my way out. It wasn't long before I could see her approaching in the distance. She wore a white skirt with a matching halter- top and a jean jacket. The word bad was a complete understatement. Melissa was sown right gorgeous. She walked up smiling.

"You look like you looking for somebody?" She looked me up and down with a smile.

"I was, but I don't see her yet, I might leave her ass." I played along. She playfully hit me.

"Boy stop playing with me." She laughed and crossed her arms over her chest.

"Naw I'm just playing. Come here." I wrapped my arms around her.

"So where are you taking me?" she asked within my embrace.

"Shit, I wanted to go to the Gucci shop, but it looks like they're closed. I sarcastically looked at my watch.

'Very funny. You got a lot of jokes Ricky Smiley."

"Naw, let's go to Denny's and get something to eat. That cool/ I looked at her.

"Yeah that's cool." She replied as I opened the car door. On the ride to Denny's the conversation went smooth. Melissa was an easy person to talk to. Her conversation was intriguing to the point I found myself hanging on her every word. Anticipating every topic, I almost wished that she didn't have to die. Soon we made it to Denny's and received our seats. It was funny that I was having a sense of Deja'vu thinking of Marcus inside IHOP. Still after our orders were placed the dialogue ensued.

"So what do you plan on doing with your life?" I asked.

"Right now, I go to American University, I'm studying Criminal Law."

"Following in her mother footsteps I see."

"Unfortunately, yeah. It's always been her dream for me to follow the foundation she laid for me."

"You sound like becoming a lawyer is something you don't want. That is a helleva accomplishment.

"I know it is, but it's her dream, not mine. I don't want to have to live a life thinking and wondering if someone I prosecuted a longtime ago is going to come back on some revenge shit. That's not a peaceful life." She explained.

'Then what are your dreams?" I asked and looked into her eyes.

"I always wanted to be a dancer." She replied looking off into space like she could see her dream manifest behind her eyes. I slightly chuckled.

"What's so funny?" She tapped me on the shoulder.

"Nothing. It's just that you have a beauty and brains. Why shake your ass, when you can make a living doing something more meaningful?"

"Just because it isn't meaningful to you, don't mean it isn't meaningful to me. That was a real inconsiderate thing to say Marcell.' I could tell that my statement pissed her off. I cursed myself. I knew I had to back pedal or risk losing my only inlet to Michelle.

"Whoa, whoa sweetheart. S first, let me apologize for speaking without clarification of my words. Never would I insinuate that your dreams and aspirations are not meaningful. If your dreams is to be a dancer, and you're my woman, then I will help you in any way that I can to obtain that. To clarify what I was saying, you're too pretty and smart to be shaking your ass when your value to the world is wroth so much more. Meaning why be the Mayor when you could be the President? Why eat a slice when you can have the whole loaf."

"I feel you Marcell, but let me clarify. I would never degrade myself by shaking my ass in some ratchet rap video. When I say dancer, I mean Choreographer. I want to teach the art. It's something I've been passionate about since I was a little girl.

"Are you familiar with the choreographer, Lurraine Gibson?" I asked. I was happy to see her demeanor change. Melissa was a sensitive spirit, I realized. From this point on, I would be sure to speak as meticulously as I could concerning her goals.

"What! Are you kidding me? Not only is she my idol, she is the biggest Hip-Hop Choreographer on the planet. I would give anything to meet that woman. She has the most juice in the industry. Period!

"I can tell. Your eyes lit up by the mention of her name." I smiled. Just the angel I was looking for.

White: Queen-C6

"Yeah I would love to meet her."

"I'm sure whatever you decide you're going to do your thing. If you let me, I'm trying to be there for you. Kind of like making your dream, my dream." I took a sip of my drink staring directly in her hazel eyes. Our gaze met one another with an electric current that burned to the point that it was met with silence as a thousand words were spoken through the flames of the current. Melissa cleared her throat with a smile. Well it's getting late, I think we should go." Melissa feebly tried to regress from the electricity that was inevitably flowing between us. I laughed at her coyness. She avoided my eye contact letting me know that she knew she had been perceived. I moved closer trapping her in the corner.

"Why are you avoiding my gaze?" Her smell was intoxicating.

"Who said I'm avoiding you?" My face was only inches from here. I spoke in a slight whisper.

"If I'm wrong, your eyes told a story of lies." I could feel her breath on my chin. I then set her top lip between mines igniting the flame that was eager to burn. Her lips were as soft as the clouds in the sky looked. It took only seconds for the sexual tension to raise enough for our hands to come alive. Each one, respectively commencing their own exploration of Melissa body. Passionately, we kissed as intimate as actual intercourse would bring. I touched her cheek as our tongues intertwined. I ran my hand under her halter-top rubbing my thumb across her nipple. She fought through the trance she fell into and placed a hand to my chest.

"That's Marcell you got that" she stated with a smile. I gave her a small peck on the forehead and smiled as well.

"Don't you ever run from me." I warned. She continued to smile. "Come on and let me get you home, Double R!" I laughed, basking in my triumph.

"Double R?" She stated in the form of confusion.

"Yeah, roadrunner!? I laughed. She playfully pinched me. We shared the laugh and were off to the Gucci shop. Although I didn't get the address, I did get something that should relieve her of any doubt she may have had about me. With that, the first bullet had been printed in the magazine.

-Chucky-

Today would be day one of my stakeout on Don. For the cause, I rented an all-white van. On the side, I had a sign made that said Your Life, My Freedom. A Second Chance at

Life. The slogan spoke volumes. A slogan that would be directly in front of Don face yet he would be blind. It would all be due to him. Also, I purchased two special twins Glock 40's with silencers equipped. I was focused to say the least, and on a mission to rectify putting Marcus's freedom in peril.

I parked on Fairmont inside the back of the van. I'd been watching DON, Head and bishop make sell after sell oblivious to the death that had them in its sights. I never been a man of patience, but this day I was forced to gain some. As I watched, I clenched one of the Glock's firmly in my palm. I was lasting patience in its pure from.

DON I saw as a straight up gangsta. What made him unique was that he was the type of gangsta that played offense and defense. He would get in the car and immediately the power locks to lock all the doors. Some would say that's a scared nigga! I'd say he was just cautious. That being, the reason why he was still alive. A move like that is no different than moving your queen back to protect the king. Every day he played to prevent himself from being checkmated.

Even with the good qualities that Don instilled in himself, he was still a man and all men have their weakness. With my extensive research on the details of DON's so called immortality, I saw his weakness to be the two men around him. DON's was immaculate, but his offense was only as strong as the three of them together. Individual, I saw the four of us as men as equal men. The trio's biggest enemy would be themselves. They had been together for so long that they knew everything about each other and their closest family members. I felt that I had a good chance to stand up under a war with them. Especially when they didn't know they were in a war. I knew it would be a trying risk, so instead of going head up, I would make him checkmate himself.

At this point in phase one Don wouldn't be the target. My eyes were set on the one who I felt was the weakest of the three. The one who I felt I could get to give any info that I would with a little pressure applied. BISHOP!

I had been watching Bishop intensely all morning. Watching him allowed me to see just how we as drug dealers make it easy for the FBI and DEA to build cases against us. I saw how money blinded us and we moved carelessly as if selling crack was legal.

Bishop was no exception and neither was Don and Head. I watched him countless times run in and out of the trap house. Blatantly, handing off packages. Throughout the day, the tri smoke, drank and sold drugs. I'd been gaining Intel now for 12 hours. It was about 9:30 pm at night. Finally, he moved toward Silver Buick Lashre. I hopped in the driver seat and immediately took up a tail, I made sure to ride pass Don thinking, His life passing before his eyes.

I followed Bishop all the way to an apartment in Prince George's country to a spot Kentland. Bishop was a relaxed individual that in the line of work he was in required you to be alert and on point. Reason being you will never know who is watching you. Bishop didn't circle the block or anything to see if he was been followed. Bishop then parked before the apartment. It was a lonely region. Only about a very few houses were located around here. He had decided to live here because he didn't want to stay where everyone would come looking at him or what he was up to. I remained at a distance, watching him pull up before the apartment. He didn't get down immediately. He remained in the car for close to ten minutes, making me wonder what he was up to. After about ten minutes, Bishop got out of the car and went into the apartment. Immediately he had into the apartment, I got out of my car and headed to the apartment.

I stood before the door. I was going to open the door, and then I heard footsteps approaching the door from the inside. I ran with the speed of light, as fast as possible, and as quiet as possible to avoid being detected. I, to cover from the building. Bishop came out of the house. He went to his car and got something that I figured out he forgot, which was now why he had to go back to the car. He looked around to make sure no one was around and within. He then walked back into the house.

I got out from where I was hiding, and I decided to move around the apartment to see if the building had any possible escape route in case things were not working as planned. When I was going around the apartment, I started hearing the splash of running water, and Bishop was taking his bath. It was the perfect moment for me to strike. I went for the door handle with just a single turn. The door was ajar. I entered quietly and found my way to the bathroom. Bishop was still in the shower when he saw a gun pointing towards him.

I wasn't in a mood to waste a single time, the business was on, but the time was far spent. "I need all there is to be known on Don and Head," I said to Bishop. He remained standing and gazing at me as if he had seen a ghost. I let a bullet out of the gun, and it went straight to his hand, he exclaimed in pain, his brain was reset, he started talking immediately. In about ten minutes, I got every information that there is to be known about Don and Head. They were not invincible after all. I left the house after placing a call to 911. They came and found Bishop lying dead with eleven bullet wounds on his body.

Don and Head had been worried since Bishop's demise became part of the daily news. There was no trace left behind for them to follow in their bid to find out who had carried the hit. They had this forthcoming deal, and it would land them a lot of money. The big issue started with Don thinking that Head was the one that murdered Bishop. They started tearing apart more than they were together. During one of their arguments, Don accused Head of killing Bishop, which further brought a lot of gap between them. They say if you want to take out an enemy that is part of a strong set, tear him out and isolate him. This was what I was able to achieve with one blow.

During one rainy night, Head was a bit drunk as he entered his car, he had been at high alert all this while, but he forgot that just one little moment of vulnerability was enough for the enemy to strike. As he got into his car to drive out of the bar premises, he felt a gun touching the back of his head. Before he could say a thing, blood was everywhere as two bullets were released into his brain.

After Head's death, it became clear to Don that he was wrong when he accused Head that he was responsible for Bishop's death. The killer was entirely someone else, someone they were never suspecting. Don became even more cautious. He never had a single place that was his permanent place of rest, and today he was here, and the next day he was there, he was moving like a rolling mause. He was able to live three whole months without being mugged because of how cautious he was. I already had the information about him. I knew all the places he would be going to, but the problem wasn't where he would be. The problem was when he would be going to those places.

It was a very cold night. Don had just got a call that his son had been kidnapped. I never wanted to play dirty with anyone's family, but this man was too difficult to go down because of his cautiousness. I only got to know he had a family through Bishop. Don had always been a man that traded in secrecy. A lot of his acquaintances never knew about his family.

Another way to successfully strike a very cautious enemy was by making him anxious and unfocused. Don had become reckless by the news of the disappearance of his son. The only place he wanted to be at around this time was beside his hidden wife. The incident was already reported to the police, and the police were doing their best to get the boy. Don had pulled up before the house as he had thrown every caution to the wind.

He was now holding the door handle when he heard a familiar voice, "Dad!" The voice said, he turned immediately, his son was running towards him, he rushed to hug his son before he could get to his son, he received thirteen bullets all over his body. It was a painful death. He wanted to hug his son so badly, but it was never happening. He fell to the ground and died immediately. I got into my car and drove out from the premises before the police could get any trace of me. As for the boy that was kidnapped, he never saw the face of the person that kidnapped him. In the end, the end became a reality.